"I'd like you to consider me as more than a friend."

Grace's breath seemed to stop for a moment, then she met his gaze. "I'm not sure what you mean by that, Simon. I wouldn't want you to think it's necessary to court me because you've landed the responsibility of looking out for me."

"That doesn't enter into it, Grace, but if you're satisfied with a friendship between us, I'll bow to your needs in this. I only want you to understand that I am very attracted to you."

Grace bowed her head, as if she would hide her face and thoughts from him. And so they sat together for long minutes, Grace seeming to soak up his warmth, Simon yearning to press his lips against her forehead.

For he was well and truly caught up in the spell of her femininity.

* * *

Saving Grace
Harlequin® Historical #1043—June 2011

Praise for
Carolyn Davidson

"Carolyn Davidson creates such vivid images, you'd think she was using paints instead of words."
—Bestselling author Pamela Morsi

"Davidson wonderfully captures gentleness in the midst of heart-wrenching challenges."
—*Publishers Weekly*

"Readers are in for a treat."
—*RT Book Reviews* on *The Bride*

"For romance centering on the joys and sorrows of married life, readers can't do much better than Davidson.... This is a sweet and sensitive novel that fulfills an evening's dreams."
—*RT Book Reviews* on *Nightsong*

"Davidson's touching western romance delivers what readers expect from a writer who strives to understand the deepest feeling and dreams of our hearts."
—*RT Book Reviews* on *Haven*

"[An] unflinching inquiry into the serious issues of the day."
—*Booklist* on *Redemption*

"Like Dorothy Garlock, Davidson does not stint on the gritty side of romance, but keeps the tender, heart-tugging aspects of her story in the forefront. This novel is filled with compassion and understanding for characters facing hardship and hatred and still finding joy in love and life."
—*RT Book Reviews* on *Oklahoma Sweetheart*

CAROLYN DAVIDSON

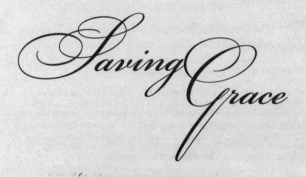

Saving Grace

TORONTO NEW YORK LONDON
AMSTERDAM PARIS SYDNEY HAMBURG
STOCKHOLM ATHENS TOKYO MILAN MADRID
PRAGUE WARSAW BUDAPEST AUCKLAND

Recycling programs
for this product may
not exist in your area.

ISBN-13: 978-0-373-29643-9

SAVING GRACE

Copyright © 2011 by Carolyn Davidson

This story is dedicated with love to a woman of faith, dignity and grace, Debbie Lindsay, a pastor's wife beyond compare, and to Mr. Ed, who loves me.

Chapter One

Maple Creek, Kansas—1890

Tears dripped to the dust beneath her feet. Small bare feet, hardly visible beneath a voluminous gray dress that clad the girl's body in an anonymous fashion. She held her hands against her cheeks, silently shielding her features from the man who seemed determined to strike her face.

His closed fist hit the side of her head, spittle flying from his mouth as he swore, harsh words that questioned her heritage, phrases that condemned her lifestyle. She fell to the ground, curling into a tight ball to shield herself against his wrath.

The rifle behind Simon's saddle had seen but little use, being carried only for his own protection as he traveled the byways of his parish, but he knew its use, and the feel of the stock in his hands was immediate as he aimed carefully at the heavyset, angry man before him. The bullet hit him, sent him spinning, and he swore ripely as he fell to the ground. Bleeding from his shoulder, he lifted his head and his cold, angry gaze touched Simon, who held his long gun ready, should he need to fire it again. The big man on the ground struggled to his feet, snatched up his hat and awkwardly gained the saddle on his mount. Within seconds he was almost lost in a cloud of dust from the dry, arid pasture that surrounded him.

Simon lifted himself quickly from his gelding and dropped the reins, knowing his horse would not stray. The girl crouched before him at the side of the road, her head bent and resting against her knees, her shoulders shuddering with the sobs she could not contain and a cloud of dark hair all but covering her face.

He dropped to one knee beside her, and his hand touched her shoulder, feeling the automatic flinch his gesture brought into being. "I won't hurt you," Simon said, his tone as gentle as he could manage, given the degree of anger he felt toward her attacker.

She lifted her head, one blue eye almost closed from the swollen flesh surrounding it. Copious amounts of crimson fell from the torn flesh of her lip to stain the front of her dress, and the fear she battled glittered in the look she slanted in his direction.

She attempted to speak, but the words were halting, garbled by the blood in her mouth, and she bent to one side and spit upon the weeds there, then sat upright and faced him with an amount of self-control he admired, even as he mourned the pain she felt.

"Who is he?" His query was harsh, but she did not withdraw from his hand on her shoulder. She seemed to recognize that his anger was directed at the man who had ridden to the north, across the open pastureland and into the edge of the wooded area beyond.

"Kenny Summers." Speaking those words seemed to have drained her strength, because she bent her head again, one hand reaching upward to touch her lower lip. Simon's stomach lurched as he saw the results of violence against the girl.

She looked up at him then, the swelling fast closing the lid of her right eye, her left fortunately untouched. "He works for my uncle and he's been after me since I've been there."

"Who's your uncle? Would I know him from town?" Simon had little hope that she could speak for long, for her mouth was already trembling from the effort she made.

"He lives on a farm about six miles south of Maple Creek. Joe Cumberland is his name, and

Kenny is one of his hired hands. He followed me this morning when I went out to the barn to milk the cow. He wouldn't leave me alone and we were by ourselves in the barn. So I swung the galvanized milk pail at him and hit him across the head with it. All I could think to do was run from him. I snatched up a bridle from a hook on the wall and caught up a mare in the corral. I put the bridle on her right quick and rode off before he could grab at me again."

She bent her head against her knees and shuddered, as if the memory of her attacker had sickened her, and Simon clenched his hand as he thought of the girl, frightened and confused, and the man who had tracked her down here.

She nodded, accepting the handkerchief he offered from his trousers' pocket. After wiping at her mouth, she looked up at Simon. "He told Uncle Joe that he wanted to marry me, last week one day. I told my uncle I wasn't ready to marry anyone and especially not Kenny. He drinks and gambles in town every chance he gets and he's mean. I couldn't bear the thought of him touching me, and when he said he'd have me one way or another, I tried to get away from him. He was mad that day, and today when he followed me to the barn and grabbed me I knew I had to get away from him.

"After I hit him with the bucket, I kicked him. He hit me then, and it was like he was crazy, just shoving me and trying to hurt me." She inhaled sharply and met his gaze again.

"He caught up with me here and I knew I was in for it. I can't tell you how glad I was to see you. You're a good shot, mister."

Simon felt an ironic smile touch his lips as he considered his next words. How to tell this girl that he was a minister, a servant of God, a man of the cloth. All neat and tidy in his good suit, going out to call on a parishioner and his ailing wife, toting a rifle behind his saddle. A man supposedly dedicated to peace and love. And yet, he'd shot a man, without thinking twice about it, had lifted his gun and put a bullet into a man's shoulder.

He laughed, a rueful sound. "I'm not really a good shot, ma'am. In this case, just lucky, I suspect. I carry the gun for protection, for I've been warned by the people in my church that this part of the country is still a bit untamed, and my safety could be in jeopardy when I ride out alone."

She stood then, looking up at him with a rare dignity he couldn't help but admire, but the expression on her face was puzzled. "I don't recognize you, mister. But I surely appreciate your help."

"I'm Simon Grafton, pastor of the Methodist church in town," he said, noting her quick smile and look of relief, as if his profession made him safe in her view.

"My name is Grace Benson," she said quietly,

pressing his handkerchief against her mouth again, then dabbing at her eyes. "My uncle took me in when my folks died a year ago. I keep house for him, and cook for his hired hands."

"And he pays you for your work?" Simon asked, recognizing that she was poorly dressed and appeared not to be the recipient of her uncle's loving care.

"No, he's given me a place to live, though," she said. Her heart pounded in her chest as she stood before the man who had come to her rescue, a tall, dark-haired stranger. Reverend Simon Grafton, he'd said.

He seemed kindly, his eyes shining upon her with a tenderness she had not expected. Men seemed to be all of a sort in her experience. Ever looking at a girl as if wondering what she would be willing to offer. But this Reverend Grafton appeared to be a different kind. Not like the men in her hometown, two of whom had been determined to possess her. She was well aware of the blessing, or perhaps curse, of having unusual beauty, for Kenny Summers was not the first man to approach her. She'd learned to repel the advances of such men over the past two years or so, fearful of all men as a result.

She clung to the assurance given her by Simon Grafton, sensing that he was not a man to be feared. She'd learned well to remain aloof to men in general, especially to Kenny Summers, he of the grasping hands and harsh, guttural words. She shivered at the thought, and Simon Grafton dropped his hand from her shoulder, then took a step toward his horse. Reaching behind his saddle he untied a rolled bit of blanket, then turned to face her once more.

"Are you cold?" he asked, unfolding the small quilt he held. He placed it around her shoulders and stepped back, as if he would not encroach on her in an unseemly manner.

She held it tightly, warming in its folds, and whispered her thanks. Then she looked up to meet his dark gaze. "I've seen you somewhere, maybe at the general store."

He whipped his hat from his head, as if recognizing that he'd neglected his manners. "That may well be, ma'am. I do my shopping there, just odds and ends mostly, for my housekeeper tends to the buying of foodstuffs."

Her sigh of relief was silent, but her heart stopped its galloping pace and settled down a bit. "I have a mare around here somewhere, but I don't know where she went when Kenny knocked me off her back. I was riding without a saddle and I slid off before I knew it." She looked around her, hoping for a glimpse of the chestnut filly she'd mounted and ridden without a second thought, so intent on fleeing Kenny's presence she hadn't properly thought out her escape from him. She might have known he'd follow her and eventually catch up.

"I feel so stupid, Mr. Grafton. I ran off without thinking, just trying to get away from Kenny, and I'd have done better to run back to the house and lock myself in. This has been a real mess, and I'll warrant my uncle is worried about me."

She eyed the man before her and then smoothed her skirts and brushed her hair back, all too aware that she hadn't taken time to braid it this morning before helping with the chores. Bad enough that she was bleeding and bruised, her clothing soiled from the dust of the road and she'd never felt so disheveled and inadequate in her life. This man, if his words were to be believed, was the local minister, and she certainly was not presenting a picture of a well-groomed woman before him.

Simon spoke quickly, his mind working at a rapid pace. "Do you want to go home? If so, I'll escort you back to your uncle's place. Or else I can take you with me to the farm where I'm scheduled to make an appearance this morning. Mr. and Mrs. Blackwood are an elderly couple who haven't been able to get out to church, what with the missus ailing. I'm on my way to visit them."

The girl seemed to deliberate for a moment and then she nodded her head, as if she had reached a decision. "I'll go with you, sir. If I go back to my uncle's, he will no doubt be out in the fields, cutting hay, and if Kenny is still around, he'll be watching for me. I don't want to see him again." As if her thoughts were chilling she shivered again within the folds of his small quilt, and Simon's heart was touched by her predicament.

"We'll go to the Blackwood farm. You can wash up a bit and later on I can let your uncle know that you're all right."

"Thank you. I don't know how to tell you how much I appreciate your going out on a limb for me this morning. I fear my uncle will not appreciate my dislike of Kenny. He wants me to be married and off his hands."

"I rather think the Blackwoods will enjoy meeting you," Simon said with a grin, thinking of the man and his wife who were without family nearby, who struggled alone on a farm with but a single hired hand to do the work in the barn.

"I'd like to go there and meet the folks and clean up a bit," the girl said, as if a decision had been made and welcomed, for her mouth curved in a smile that held appreciation for his efforts.

"Well, Miss Grace, let's take a ride together," Simon said, his voice quiet, as if he would comfort her. "I don't see your horse anywhere around. I think you're right, for she must have bolted, maybe even run off back home, when you fell from her back. If you don't mind riding double, my horse will bear the load easily."

He mounted his gelding and reached down for her hand, lifting her easily to sit astride behind himself. From the corner of his eye, he watched her smooth her skirts over her legs as much as possible and then he slid his rifle into the scabbard, slipping it beneath her leg until it was lodged in place.

"Are you hanging on tight?" he asked, feeling her hands clutching at his suit coat.

"Can I reach beneath and hold on to your belt?"

He smiled, recognizing that she was embarrassed by her own plea, then removed his suit coat and folded it over his lap, offering the leather belt he wore as a handhold for her.

He pressed his heels to the gelding's sides and his horse set off at a quick pace, seemingly not even aware of the extra weight on his back. Simon's thoughts were filled with the slight figure of the woman who sat behind him, whose dark hair fell loosely about her shoulders and down her back. She was a young woman of perhaps twenty or so, he thought, and to that end asked a question.

"How old are you, Grace? How did your parents die and leave you alone at such a young age?"

"They were killed in a fire in our house while I was gone with a friend for an overnight visit a year ago. I was almost twenty, but was still living at home. I'd been helping my mother run the house for several years, since I graduated from the school in town. Mama wasn't well, and I pretty much did everything for her and my daddy. He ran the hardware store in town. Not in Maple Creek, but east of here, in Mill Springs, where the big sawmill is. I'd never been out of the area till my folks died and my Uncle Joe came to the funeral and took me home with him. He handled all the financial matters for me, took care of everything. He's all the family I have, my mother's brother."

And not much in the way of a protector, Simon thought silently, given his inability to keep watch over a young, vulnerable woman. Yet, he forbade himself to speak disparagingly of the man, not willing to insult him without knowing more about the circumstances.

"I think you'd do well to stay away from your uncle's place for a while, at least until he is made aware of Kenny Summer's attack on you, and the sheriff notified."

He felt her grip tighten on his belt as she huddled closer to his back, her warm breath reaching him even through the fabric of his shirt. Simon was at a loss as to what he would do with the girl. She seemed relaxed a bit behind him, and he felt the weight of her head as she leaned against his back. He felt drawn to her. Perhaps it was even a physical sort of attraction, yet one that went deeper, more of a need to know her better, to come to realize the strength and courage she possessed.

He felt a stirring within himself he did not welcome, for he would not frighten her, and yet his body responded, as though she were sent to him in some way. And wasn't that a foolish thought, for who would have known he was traveling the town road today, and how could the girl have chanced to be in need of rescue? Yet the thought nagged at him, his mother's words repeating themselves over in his mind.

"It's time for you to be finding a wife and having a family of your own, Simon. I'm praying that God will send you the right woman."

She'd ended her last letter to him with those words, and he grinned as he thought of what his mother would say now, should she see him with this young woman clutching his belt as she rode behind him this morning.

He made an effort then to clear his thoughts as they rode silently, his horse moving at a rolling canter as they approached the homestead where the Blackwoods lived. A small farmhouse lay at the end of a long lane, with a barn and chicken coop behind it and a garden nestled beside the house.

"We're here, Grace." Simon's words were quiet, his horse slowing as they approached the back of the house where a hitching post offered a place to tie his horse.

He felt her weight slide from behind him and he reached to grasp her waist with one long arm, guiding her to the ground, lest she fall. Then, with a quick movement, he dismounted and tied his gelding to the metal ring provided for the purpose.

Grace stood beside him, trying in vain to smooth the fabric of her dress, reaching to touch the bruising on her face, which was fast becoming more painful. She lifted her fingers, feeling a welt that circled one eye and swelling on her jaw. Her mouth, too, had swollen in a startling manner.

"Well, hello there, Pastor Grafton," the kindly farmer who had come to the door said. "Looks like you've got a problem here. Have you been set upon by a gang of ruffians, miss?" He stepped closer to the pair who stood on his porch. His face showed concern as he looked into Grace's battered features.

"One ruffian, and a nasty one at that," Simon said. "He assaulted Miss Benson. I came upon them by the side of the road and I'm afraid I lost my temper and put a bullet in the man's shoulder. He rode off and I felt Miss Benson would do well to come along with me this morning. I hope you don't mind having an extra visitor."

"Come in. Come in," Mr. Blackwood said, holding the screen door wide to allow them to walk into the kitchen. "The missus is having a cup of tea, ma'am. Perhaps you'd like to join her."

"That would be most welcome."

Grace sat down at the table, her gaze on the

woman who watched her with concern. Her right arm in a sling, her face careworn, Mrs. Blackwood still managed a smile of welcome as she approached Grace.

"Harold, get the girl a warm cloth to wipe her face with," Mrs. Blackwood told her husband, and then reached for Grace's hand. She watched as her husband did as instructed, keeping an eagle eye on Grace as she wiped at her face, wincing as the cloth touched the torn flesh.

"I'll give you one of my old dresses and you can change out of that ripped one you're wearing," Mrs. Blackwood said, rising and motioning Grace to follow her. They went into a bedroom just down the hall and Mrs. Blackwood reached into her wardrobe and pulled forth a gray cotton dress that had seen better days.

"Don't worry about bringing this back to me. I haven't worn it in quite a spell and I won't miss it," the kindly lady said, and Grace thanked her, stripping from her own torn dress and donning the one offered in its stead.

"You look like you could use a bit of comfort, girl," she said, reaching with her good left arm to pat at Grace's shoulder as they returned to the kitchen.

"Here, Harold," Mrs. Blackwood said to her husband. "Pour some of that hot water into the teapot, why don't you, and I'll add some more tea leaves. Should have a cup brewing in no time at all." Within minutes the tea was poured and Grace was sipping awkwardly at the hot drink, lifting the cup to her mouth. It indeed appeared to be nourishing, for she began speaking to the lady of the house in an undertone, telling Mrs. Blackwood of her trying circumstances.

"Dear girl, don't you worry a bit," that lady said, concern for the younger woman apparent in her eyes and the tender smile she offered.

"I came to see how you were doing, Mrs. Blackwood," Simon said. "The ladies from church said they'd sent some stew and fresh bread out the other day. Is there anything else you can think of that they can do for you? Perhaps a cake or a nice roast for your dinner tomorrow? If you're needing anything from the general store just give me a list and I'll tend to it."

His offer was met with an outstretched hand from Harold and a genuine word of thanks from his wife. "Folks have been right good to us," Harold said, waving at an array of dishes on the kitchen dresser. "We've emptied all of those already, but a nice roast would tide us over well for a couple of days."

"I'd thought to leave Grace here with you folks for a day or so, but I've been thinking it over," Simon said slowly. "Perhaps she would be safer in town, close to the sheriff and where I can keep a good eye on her. How about it, Grace? I have a housekeeper living in the parsonage, so you'd have another woman in the house and that should stave off any gossip about you being there."

"I'll do whatever you decide is best," Grace said quietly, her hands clasping together, her eyes falling to the floor. "I wouldn't want Kenny to come here thinking I was on the premises. He's a dangerous man. And I wouldn't want to cause any problems for these folks."

Harold spoke up then. "I think you're right, Preacher. The girl would be welcome here, but the safer place for her and for us, too, might be if she went to town with you. There's folks all around and she could get help in a hurry if she needed it."

"I think that's decided, then, Grace. We'll leave these folks for now, as soon as I speak with Ellie for a moment, and I'll take you home with me."

Grace walked out onto the porch after offering her goodbyes to the couple and Harold followed her there. "The preacher will take good care of you, girl. He's got a fine lady for a housekeeper and you'll be safe with him."

"I'll do whatever he thinks best, sir," Grace said softly.

Behind them the door opened and Simon stepped out onto the porch. "We'll be on our way, Harold. I'll bring back the things Ellie needs from the general store one day this week. Probably the day after tomorrow, if that's all right. For now, I'll take Grace home with me and get her settled in."

Harold reached for Simon's hand and shook it, his smile wide as he heard Simon's words. The horse waited patiently at the hitching rail, and Simon went to him, Grace behind him. He mounted and then took her by the waist, lifting her to sit across his lap.

"This might be more comfortable for you, I think," he said to her, watching as she arranged her skirts to cover her legs. Harold grinned at them, waving a farewell as he went back into the house, neither of the men aware of the silent rider slouched over his saddle horn as he watched from the edge of the woods.

Simon held Grace with care as the horse set off down the lane to the town road. He did not want to alarm her by his grip on her body. Grace. What an apt name for a lovely young woman, he mused. Even given the bruises she wore, he had caught a glimpse of the gentle lines of her face, her clear skin where it was visible and the stunning blue of her eyes.

"I hope your housekeeper won't mind that I'm invading her territory," Grace said, shifting to look up at Simon.

He smiled at her, his heart strangely warmed by the woman he held in his arms. He'd not been this close to a female in three years, not since his arrival in town as the new minister, and yet it seemed like a natural thing to hold her thusly, her head against his shoulder, her body close to his.

"Mrs. Anderson will be happy to have the company, I'm sure. Keeping house for me is her job, but she's also a friend of mine, and I'm sure you'll like her."

The ride back to town was accomplished in short order and Simon quietly pointed out the various places Grace might be interested in as they passed by the business establishments on the main street. The parsonage sat next to the small church and he directed the horse around the yard and to the back door before he lifted Grace from his lap and lowered her to stand on the ground.

She brushed down her dress and watched as he dismounted and tied his mount to a handy post there. The door opened and a lady stood within the kitchen, a frown furrowing her brow as she eyed the girl before her.

"Ethel, this is Grace. She'll be with us for a bit. She's had some trouble befall her this morning. A man from her uncle's ranch chased her down and was giving her a bad time when I rode up and saw them. I stopped in at Harold and Ellie's place for a bit and then brought Grace home with me."

"Well, you come right in here where it's comfortable, girl. Let me take a look at you and see what we can do about your face."

Chapter Two

Grace looked at Simon and he smiled at her encouragingly, ushering her into the kitchen. Pulling a chair from the round, oak table, he offered her a seat and she settled down to await Ethel's ministrations.

She looked around the comfortable kitchen, to the stove where a kettle full of some concoction simmered, with an aroma she could barely resist. "What are you cooking?" she asked Ethel.

"Just some soup for dinner. I'll bet you're hungry, Grace. We'll put an extra bowl on the table for you. I always cook plenty so there's leftovers. The reverend here comes in at odd hours sometimes and it pays to have soup ready for him."

"Is the guest room ready for a visitor, Ethel?" Simon asked quietly.

Ethel nodded. "I put clean sheets in there when the bishop left last week. It's all ready for company."

"I'll show Grace where it is, then, and get her settled before dinner. She'll probably want to wash up a bit and see to her cut lip."

"I'll come up with the box of bandages and salves," Ethel offered.

Simon cast her a look of appreciation as he led Grace from the kitchen, through the hallway and up the open stairway. She followed, her hand on his arm as they climbed the stairs and passed by two closed doors before he opened the third and stood back for her to walk into the room.

It was large and sunny, with white lace curtains and colorful braided rugs on the floor. A patchwork quilt covered the bed and fat pillows leaned against the headboard.

"This is lovely," Grace said, standing in the middle of the room and looking around at the furniture it held. A wide dresser with mirror attached stood between the windows and a screen shielded one corner of the room from view.

"There's a commode back there with a pitcher and a bowl handy for you to use. I'll take the pitcher down and fill it with warm water from the stove for you and give you a few minutes to wash up and tend to your bruises. Ethel will be up here before you know it, anyway," Simon said, stepping behind the screen and reappearing in seconds with the blue-flowered pitcher.

He left the room and Grace took a look at the private place provided. A cabinet held a covered jar for nighttime use and there were towels and wash-cloths on a shelf. She found it hard to believe that she'd been given so nice a place to stay, but then realized that the parsonage must be well equipped for company.

The bedroom door opened again and Ethel came in, a shoe box in one hand, the pitcher of water in the other. Grace walked to where she stood near the bed.

"Why don't you sit down here and let me take a look at you. I'll get the towel and washcloth and you just rest a minute," Ethel said, bending to inspect Grace's face. She tutted over the bruising around the girl's eye, exclaimed loudly as she noted the cuts on her lip and the blood that seeped from her cheek.

"That rascal needs to be horsewhipped, treating a lady this way," Ethel said, her anger at the absent Kenny spoken loudly.

"He's not a nice man. But my uncle thinks he's a good worker and apparently that's all that counts with him," Grace said quietly, lifting her face for Ethel's inspection.

A jar of salve was brought forth from the box and once Ethel had washed the blood from Grace's skin, she set about soothing the sore places with her supply of ointments. In ten minutes, she had washed and cleaned all the sore spots, put a bit of sticky plaster on one cut that required it and then stepped back to look at her work.

"I think we've done all we can for right now, Grace. You may have to let the doctor take a look at you, but I think just a bit of salve every day for a week should solve most of your problems. I'm sure you'll have a black eye, but there doesn't seem to be any lasting damage."

"I can't thank you enough, Ethel. I appreciate all you and the preacher are doing for me. I didn't expect to be in such a fine house with people to care about me."

"Well, our Simon is a good man and he'll be sure you're safe here. I'll guarantee it, for I keep a shotgun in the pantry and I know how to use it if need be," Ethel said stoutly.

Grace lifted herself from her seat on the bed. "I need to wash my hands and arms before I eat any soup," she said, heading for the corner where the warm water and bowl awaited her. Ethel nodded and gathered up her supplies in the box, then went to the bedroom door.

"You come on down when you're ready, girl. Soup's ready to eat, so I'll give you ten minutes or so to finish up here."

Grace nodded and bent to the washbasin provided for her, splashing water on her hands and using another clean cloth to wash her arms. She was skinned in several places, but otherwise found no need for worry. Wiping her arms carefully with the towel provided, she dried her hands and then went to the dresser to take a look at her face.

Ethel had done a good job of cleaning her up, she decided, eyeing the skin that was bruised and the cuts that would take time to heal. Straightening her borrowed clothing as best she could, she left the room and went down the stairs to the sound of voices in the kitchen.

Simon sat at the table, rising when Grace came in the door. "Have a seat, won't you, Grace?" he asked, pulling out the same chair she'd occupied earlier.

She did as he said and watched as Ethel filled the bowls from the big kettle on the stove. The soup steamed and sent forth a scent of chicken broth, making Grace's mouth water, for she hadn't eaten yet today. She waited until Ethel sat down and lifted her napkin to spread it over her lap.

Simon bent his head and Grace was quick to do the same, as Ethel folded her hands and awaited Simon's words of prayer over the food. Another welcome idea for Grace, for she hadn't heard grace spoken over a meal since her parents' deaths a year ago. It warmed her heart that this household should be so like the home she'd lived in for her youth and childhood.

"Eat hearty now, Grace," Simon said with a smile. "My Ethel is a good cook, as you'll find out."

"The soup is wonderful," Grace said, savoring her first bite of chicken and noodles.

"We'll have you looking hale and hearty in no time," Ethel said, passing a plate of bread to the girl across the table. A plate with a round of butter on it was before her, and a bowl of jam beside it tempted her to use both on her bread. Grace could not believe her good fortune, when just a few hours ago she'd feared she might die at the hands of Kenny Summers.

"I can't tell you how thankful I am for all the two of you are doing for me," she said, her hands busy with the knife as she buttered her bread.

"We'll keep you safe until the sheriff can take care of the man who hurt you," Simon said. "I'll go and see him as soon as we're done eating and let him know what's happened."

"Will he need to talk to me?" Grace asked.

"I'm sure he will, but he's a good fellow. Perhaps he'll come by this afternoon and hear what you have to say. I'll tell him what happened but he'll no doubt want to speak with you, too."

Grace nodded in agreement, and lifted her spoon again.

* * *

Simon left after his dinner and untied his horse from the post by the back door, mounting and heading for the sheriff's office. When he got there, he tied his gelding to the rail before the jailhouse and mounted the step, opening the door and calling out to the lawman who sat at his desk.

Charlie Wilson was a man of middle age and few words. He responded to Simon's greeting with an outstretched hand and a nod, then uttered the pleasantries.

"Hello there, Reverend. This is a surprise. What can I do for you?"

Simon nodded. "A surprise visit for me, also, but I come with news that will not be to your liking, I fear. I'm upset at it myself, and decided you needed to be aware of happenings." Charlie sat down, leaning back in his chair, his feet propped on the corner of his desk, and waved at a second seat before the desk. Simon sat quickly, sorting through the words he had chosen with which to speak his piece.

"I need to let you know that there was an altercation outside town today, Sheriff. I was riding out to visit with parishioners and came upon a man abusing a young woman by the side of the road. He had bloodied her face and as I neared, he hit her in the side of the head with his closed fist. The fact is…I shot him."

Charlie's feet hit the floor with a thud and he

stood, leaning over his desk. "You killed the fella? I haven't heard of any such thing, Preacher. There's been no talk around town, at least."

"No, sir. I only shot him in the shoulder, but he got on his horse and rode off. He's a man named Kenny Summers, and I understand he works for a fella called Joe Cumberland."

"I know Joe. He's a good man. A bit hardheaded and cranky, but an honest citizen. Can't figure out why he'd have hired on a man with a temper like that." He looked squarely into Simon's eyes and asked the question that logically came next.

"Who was the woman? Somebody from town?"

"No such thing. She's Joe Cumberland's niece, Grace Benson. She said she's been living with her uncle since her folks died in a house fire a year or so ago. Seems that Kenny Summers was hot on her tracks, wanting to marry her and she wasn't interested. He made advances to her and she smacked him with a milk pail this morning and ran off on one of Cumberland's mares. When Kenny caught her he was madder than a hornet and hauled her off the mare and—well, who knows what he had in mind for the girl. Whatever he'd planned to do to her, he didn't get a chance for more than some slaps and a punch that bloodied her up. I drew my rifle out from behind my saddle and fired at him."

Charlie grinned widely. "I never had a preacher

in one of my jail cells before. Not that I'm gonna do such a thing today, Reverend. Sounds to me like you were within your rights. Hell, there's men in town who'd say you shoulda killed him where he stood. There's no excuse for a man hitting a woman, no matter what."

The sheriff reached for his gun belt, hanging on a coatrack behind his desk, then buckled it below his waist and took the gun he usually carried from a desk drawer. After checking the bullets within, he shoved it into his holster.

"Guess I'll take me a little ride out to Joe Cumberland's place and see if I can find this Summers fella. I wonder if he came to town to see Doc Henderson with his bullet wound. Maybe I'll check there first." He looked up at Simon then, suppressing a chuckle. "I'll bet he didn't tell him who shot him, if that was the case."

Simon shrugged. "I felt I needed to let you know what happened, Charlie."

The sheriff paused, halfway out the door. "What did you do with the girl?"

"I took her home with me. My housekeeper is looking after her, and I doubt that anyone will be seeking her out at my house. I'll keep an eye on her for a while, till she decides what she wants to do."

"You gonna let her uncle know where she is?" Charlie asked him.

Simon dithered a bit at that. "Haven't decided yet. He'll probably be worried about her. Maybe I should let him know she's all right."

"Then again," Charlie said slowly, "the man don't seem to take very good care of his responsibilities if he left her wide-open to Summers's attentions. Joe Cumberland is a good man, but he's harsh, tends to be nasty-tempered. Maybe the girl's better off if he doesn't know where she is."

"I doubt that Kenny has darkened my church door, so he may not have recognized me," Simon said.

"Just let it ride for now, and I'll drop by to see her later on," the sheriff said, his brow furrowed.

"I'll take your advice," Simon told him, walking out the door to the street. "If you need to see me, you know where I live." He mounted his gelding and turned back toward the parsonage. He'd do well to put Grace out of his mind for the afternoon. He had a sermon to prepare for Sunday and it was going to be a tough one to preach. He'd been doing a series on the Ten Commandments, and this week he was scheduled to use "Thou shalt not kill" as his sermon topic.

He thought of the anger he'd felt so vividly when he'd lifted his gun against Kenny Summers. For the second time in his life, the urge to kill had certainly been in his heart. And remembering the last time such an emotion had clutched at him, he lost himself in the memory that lived forever in the back of his mind.

It was something he'd had to deal with for almost ten years, a sin he'd committed and then confessed, his soul being absolved from the stain, even though his mind still clung to those moments when he'd taken a life. The man had been a threat to Simon's mother, a roughneck who'd entered their home and had the brazenness to approach his mother in her kitchen, threatening her with bodily harm. Simon, barely dry behind the ears, as his mother was fond of saying, had come in the back door, and before his anger could be curbed, he'd taken down the shotgun his father kept over the door and shot the man where he stood.

Since that moment he'd grieved over the stain on his own soul. The sheriff had absolved him of a crime, his pastor had firmly stood behind him during the hearing that followed and his family had called him blessed for defending his mother. And yet, he'd carried the guilt of taking a man's life, had gone through the years of university and seminary trying in vain to forget his part in the death of a fellow human being.

And now he faced again the memory of lifting a weapon against a man, of wishing, if only for those few seconds, that Kenny Summers would not live to see another day. And for that, he must seek absolution in some way.

He rode slowly to the church where he kept an office, dismounting from his gelding, his mind filled with the work ahead of him. He opened the back entrance to the church and stepped into his study, taking a seat behind the large desk he'd inherited along with the position he'd taken here in Maple Creek, Kansas.

From his desk drawer he drew forth a list of notes he'd made for his sermon, and spent the next fifteen minutes reading them over, in vain seeking a way to put together the sermon he would give on Sunday. To no avail, for before his eyes was the vision of a young woman with blue eyes and dark hair. A woman who might be sleeping, even now, in the extra room at his house. For Grace Benson had been foremost in his every thought since the moment he'd first seen her, and if ever there was a young woman who appealed to his masculine nature, it was Grace.

He inhaled sharply, banishing her from his mind, concentrating instead on the sermon he must prepare. He opened his Bible before him on his desk and sought out the passages he would use. His heart was heavy within him, for he felt the overwhelming sense of guilt once more.

Thou shalt not kill. Not that he'd done such a thing, but certainly the thought of delivering death to the man this morning had been in his mind. He'd aimed purposely for Kenny Summers's shoulder, but the urge to lift his sights to the man's head had tempted him.

A classic sin, one of murder. For it would have been just that. Summers had not flaunted a gun, had been unarmed, but for the fists he had used on the girl. And for that, he'd deserved death in Simon's mind. And that was the thought he could not relinquish.

There was no chance of skipping this commandment and going on to the next. His congregation knew all too well the order in which those Holy words had been written centuries ago. It was his task to deliver a sermon from a mind that had known the urge to kill, thus breaking the very commandment he must expound upon.

Soon his thoughts were filled with the knowledge of Moses and those who were wandering in the wilderness in Bible days. The words came to him as he studied and he wrote industriously on his paper, putting the thoughts that bloomed within his mind onto the written page. Amid his studying, he spent long moments dealing with his own behavior of the morning, finding it in his heart to forgive himself for the emotion he'd felt toward the man beside the road. The sermon finished, at least the rough draft of it, he prepared to leave his office.

He lifted the Bible he'd used from the table, deposited it on the shelf in his study and made his way back to the parsonage. And to Grace.

Chapter Three

Sheriff Charlie Wilson appeared at the parsonage the next morning, doffing his hat as Ethel Anderson opened the door to him.

"Good morning, ma'am. I've come to see your houseguest, if I may."

Ethel smiled and ushered the lawman into the parlor. "I'll see if Grace is ready for visitors, sir," she said, leaving the caller ensconced on the horsehair sofa. In moments, she'd located Grace in her bedroom and escorted her to the parlor, introducing the sheriff with a few chosen words.

Grace, previously warned by Simon that the lawman might seek her out, was cordial. "Good morning, Sheriff. I suspected you'd be coming by to see me."

Charlie's gaze touched upon Grace's face, and he

looked uncomfortable, clearing his throat noisily before he replied. "Well, according to your uncle, his ranch hand is making a charge against the Reverend. Kenny Summers says our preacher tried to kill him for no reason yesterday. I let Joe Cumberland know I was aware of the circumstances and asked to see the man, but to no avail, for he could not be found while I was there. I had intended to question him about his actions where you were concerned, Miss Benson. Your uncle denied that his ranch hand had done anything to harm you, but I can see from the looks of you that he obviously hasn't seen your face. I'm assuming that your black eye was at Kenny Summers's hand, ma'am," the sheriff said, his keen eyes searching Grace's features.

"Joe said the man had followed you because he was fearful for your safety, riding out alone the way you did. But I find that a bit difficult to believe."

A door banging at the back of the house announced Simon's entry and in mere moments he appeared in the parlor doorway. "I thought I heard your voice, Sheriff," he said. "I see you've met Miss Benson, sir." Doffing his hat as he made his way to where Grace stood, he grinned widely. "Can I assume you're not here to arrest me?"

"I've seen your houseguest and I'm satisfied that the man in question deserved more than a bullet in the shoulder."

The sheriff turned to Grace then, speaking kindly to her, as if he feared upsetting her. "I need to know just what happened yesterday, young lady. Would you care to tell me about it?"

"Yes, sir. I lost out in a fuss with Kenny Summers." She quickly recounted the details of her ordeal with the man, feeling a blush rise to cover her cheeks as she thought of Kenny's hands on her arms, of his fleshy lips nearing her own as he'd bent to speak with her and kiss her in the barn that morning.

Grace looked into the lawman's gaze then, wanting to emphasize her position. "I didn't like Kenny. I didn't want him touching me, and I sure didn't want him courting me, and I told him so." She paused, lifting her gaze to touch that of Simon, who watched and waited as she spoke.

Charlie Wilson spoke quickly then. "No need to say anything more, Miss Benson. I understand what you're telling me. Just quickly give me the details of your leaving your uncle's ranch."

In a few short words she gave him chapter and verse of her flight from Kenny and the following minutes by the side of the road when he pulled her from the mare. "He said I needed to learn a lesson and he was just the one to teach me. His fist clobbered me under my eye and a couple of other places, too."

Her hand lifted in an automatic gesture to touch

the swelling where hard knuckles had caught her cheekbone, and she noted the flinch the sheriff could not conceal.

"He had no right to touch you, Miss Benson," Charlie said, his tone harsh as he cleared his throat.

Grace tried to smile, but her lips would not form the expression. "I didn't think so, either, but he was madder than ever when I told him so. That was when the preacher rode up and saw Kenny punch me. I turned my head a bit and he missed my other eye that time, but just about knocked me out, smacking the side of my head with his fist.

"When he saw the preacher's gun pointed at him, he was really mad and I don't think he gave the preacher enough credit, for he laughed as if he didn't have anything to fear. When he started toward me again, I heard the gun fire and Kenny had blood running from his shoulder. He grabbed up his horse and was gone."

"Well, that's pretty much what I expected to hear," Charlie said, nodding at Grace as if he accepted her words as the truth. "Did Kenny threaten you with a gun, or just his fists?"

"I don't think he wanted to kill me, Sheriff, just let me know who was boss. He wasn't carrying a gun so far as I know," Grace said.

Charlie laughed a bit, his grin seemingly aimed

at Simon. "Guess he found out who was in charge after all, didn't he?"

Grace spoke up softly. "I don't know what I'd have done if Pastor Grafton hadn't come along when he did. I'm sure things would not have ended so well."

"I think you're right, Miss Benson," Charlie said. He stood then and nodded at the man who sat beside Grace. "I'll take my leave, Reverend. I've heard all I need to know from this young lady. There won't be any charges filed in any official way against you. In fact, once I can locate him, I'll be bringing Kenny Summers into the jail and holding him there on charges of assault toward this young lady."

"My uncle won't be happy with that. He'll be short a man, and he seems to have a hard time keeping ranch hands on the place as it is," Grace said quickly.

"To tell the truth, miss, I really don't care about your uncle's bad temper and the fact he can't keep his crew happy. This man is going to jail and when Judge Henry Hale comes through on his regular schedule, Kenny will face him. He may require your presence there to testify, if you don't mind."

Grace shook her head. "I'll appear if necessary."

Simon followed the sheriff out the door and shook his hand. "I hope you'll cut Grace a bit of slack. Facing that fellow again would just open up the whole attack in her mind, I fear. She's really frightened of him and, given his size, I can't blame her."

Charlie halted just below the porch, nodding in understanding. "I'll do what I can. And I'd say you'll do well to keep a close watch on that young lady, Reverend. She'd make a fine addition to your parsonage, I'd say. You ever thought about getting married?" His grin was wide as the lawman spoke and Simon felt the man had almost read his thoughts.

But that the sheriff should be so blunt, inquiring about his personal feelings, was a surprise, and Simon turned a sober face to him, hoping that his discomfort was not noticeable. "A man would have to be blind not to notice her pretty dark hair and blue eyes. She's a lovely woman and if I were in the market for a wife, I'd no doubt be looking in her direction." He felt a rush of blood to his cheeks as he spoke and noted the quick grin the lawman tossed his way.

"And you're not looking?" Charlie asked with a smile that sat well upon his kindly face.

"Haven't given it much thought. But my mother sure thinks I oughta be on the lookout for a wife. She says I shouldn't wait much longer before starting a family. I hear the same story every time she writes me a letter."

Charlie laughed aloud. "That sure enough sounds like a mother to me." And then he sobered. "Might be a good idea to consider the girl, Reverend. She needs a soft place to land and you could do a whole lot worse than to court her a bit, see if she suits you. A congregation likes having a woman in the parsonage, and not just a housekeeper, either. Every man needs a good wife behind him, and I'd think a preacher man might be even more in need of a companion."

"Thanks for the advice, Charlie," Simon said, allowing his mind to focus on the girl they discussed. She was well worth getting to know better, he decided, and Charlie might have hit upon a solution to Grace's problems.

It was worth thinking about. Not that his thoughts had strayed far from Grace Benson over the past day; even now they were thoroughly enmeshed in the young woman under his roof as he watched the sheriff take his leave.

The parlor was empty when Simon went back into the house, so he headed to the kitchen, seeking out Grace, needing to speak with her. He found her standing before the sink, rinsing soap from the last of the breakfast dishes, and he spoke her name, gaining her attention. She turned to him, dish towel in hand.

"Yes, Simon. Did you need to talk with me?"

His sharp eyes met hers then and she turned

away, seeming embarrassed by the long minutes he spent looking at her.

"Don't conceal your face from me, Grace. I have no doubt but what your features will be as pleasing as ever, given a day or two to recover from Kenny's blows. In fact, I find you more than lovely as you are."

She looked up quickly, as if unbelieving of his words. "I know what I look like, sir. I have a mirror in the room you gave me."

"Well, don't think for a minute there's anything about you that would make me hesitate to call you lovely, Grace. I can see beyond the marks on your face, and I suspect that there is a most becoming young woman before me. I'd like to know you better, in fact."

"I don't want your congregation to think badly of you, sir, letting me stay here in your home. They might not appreciate it."

He shook his head. "It's my Christian duty after all, Grace. You have a place to stay in this house as long as you need to. Ethel is a fit chaperone for any young woman, and my congregation will be aware of that. Don't think you'll be causing me any harm by sleeping in my spare room. I've already spoken to a couple of the men from my congregation and they seemed to agree that it was fitting for you to be here."

"Thank you, Simon. I can't tell you how much

it means to have a room where I can be safe. I appreciate it more than you know."

He watched as she hung the dish towel by the oven, and then he waved a hand at the back door. "Do you suppose we could go out and sit on the step and talk for a while?"

Grace hesitated but a moment and then a smile lit her features.

"I'd like that, Simon." She walked before him to the door and stepped out onto the porch, settling on the top step as he moved to sit beside her. His hands fell between his knees as he leaned forward, elbows on his thighs.

"I'd like to know more about you, Grace. Did you have a happy childhood? Were your parents young?"

"I was probably spoiled," she said after a moment's thought. "I was all they had and my father was good to both my mother and me. He had a hardware business, and he and my mother were popular with the folks around town. My father was a kind man, with a good word for everyone, and my mother was happy with him. Once I graduated school, I thought about getting a job as a clerk in the local emporium, but my father said he'd rather have me at home, helping Mama with the housework and such."

"Did your parents take you to church?" Simon asked, curious as to her religious background.

"Oh, yes, I went to Sunday school and church alike. And to Vesper services on Sunday nights. Mama sang in the choir and Daddy was so proud of her." Her voice caught on the final words she spoke, and Simon caught a glimpse of tears on her cheek.

"I'm sorry, Grace. I didn't mean to bring back memories that would upset you," he said, his hand touching her shoulder, and then falling away, as if he feared being too forward.

She turned to him quickly. "Oh, no. I'm not upset about my memories, but I find I still tend to be a bit weepy when I talk about my family. It was awfully hard to accept that they were gone after the fire, and I truly grieved, knowing I'd never see them again. If I hadn't been visiting with my friend, who knows what might have happened to me, for I'd have been caught by the flames, too."

"There's a reason for everything that happens, Grace," Simon told her, his arm lifting to enclose her shoulders as she wept. "We may not understand why things happen the way they do, but I'm a firm believer that there is a plan for each of our lives, and that ultimately, we have no control over those things that change our circumstances."

She turned her head and her gaze touched his. "Thank you, Simon. I appreciate your kindness. I have good memories about my family and our home, and I try to concentrate on those instead of mourning."

"You're a brave girl. You have my admiration," he said, his big hand squeezing her shoulder in comfort. "I find myself drawn to you, Grace. I don't want to be too bold or forward with you, but I must tell you that you appeal to me on many levels. In fact, I'd like you to consider me as more than a friend."

Her breath seemed to stop for a moment, as if she were stunned, and then she lifted her head, her gaze meeting his for a moment. "I'm not sure what you mean by that, Simon, but I'd think being friends would be best for both of us right now. I would hope I haven't placed you in an uncomfortable position. I wouldn't want you to feel obligated to me, or think it's necessary to court me because you've been landed with the responsibility of looking out for me."

"That doesn't enter into it, Grace, but if you're satisfied with a friendship between us, I'll bow to your needs in this. Just know that I would never choose a wife strictly because I felt a responsibility toward her," Simon said quietly. "I only want you to understand that I admire you, that I am very attracted to you. My mother has long been after me to find a wife, and until now I've not seen a woman who appealed to me as a bride. Not until I brought you into my home and found that you fit well here. I won't tell you I'm in love with you for I have no intention of lying to you in any way. But I can say, very truthfully, that you make me yearn to know you better. I fear I'm smitten with you, as the ladies back home used to say when a young man trailed around behind a young lady and obviously admired her."

Grace chuckled softly at his words, her head bowed, as if she would hide her face and thoughts from him. And so they sat together for long minutes, Grace seeming to soak up his warmth, Simon aching to bend closer to the girl beside him, yearning to press his lips against her forehead, longing to touch the fine skin of her temple. For he was well and truly caught up in the spell of her femininity. As if she were meant to be in his life at this time and in this place, he felt a kinship with her. But as he'd told her, if friendship was what she wanted from him, he would oblige her.

She looked up at him and her smile was once more that which he'd seen before: a welcoming gesture of warmth he accepted gladly. "I appreciate you, Simon. And Ethel, as well. She's a nice lady and she's been ever so kind. She brings to mind my aunt Sadie, my father's sister, who died several years ago. When I saw Ethel, it made me feel somehow as if I'd come home again."

"That's how I want you to feel, Grace. As though this place is home to you. If you decide to do otherwise than to stay here, sometime in the future, it will be all right, but for now, I want you to consider this your home. If you want to go back to your uncle Joe's place sometime to visit, I'll take you. But you're welcome here. I hope you know that."

She sighed. "I do. I really do. And I don't know if I could ever go back to Uncle Joe's ranch. I felt like a fish out of water there, with all those menfolk around and only a housekeeper to speak with. I'd feel more comfortable if he came to see me here."

Simon's heart lifted, and he couldn't help but smile at her. She was so honest and forthright, so open in her words and actions. He hadn't been impressed with a woman to this extent in a long time.

For even in his younger years, his thoughts had been on his education, not the females in his circle. But not so, now. So he spoke quickly, before he lost his courage.

"I have to tell you that I'm drawn to you, Grace, as a man is to a woman he'd like to court. I know we haven't had any time together to speak of, hardly know each other really, but I'm a man who makes up his mind in a hurry. And I've seemed to settle on you. You are all I've ever looked for in a woman, and I want you to know that my thoughts are centered on making you a part of my life. Can you consider it, having known me for mere days? Am I rushing you too much, or perhaps frightening you?"

She shook her head. "No, you don't frighten me. Perhaps I've also looked for a person I could come to care for. You are a wonderful man, Simon, and I feel…fond of you already. Just know that I have no fear of your feelings and I'll consider you in that light."

He smiled, a warmth radiating from his face as he spoke. "It's exactly what I have in mind, Grace." He bent then, his mouth touching her brow, sliding to her temple and thus to her cheek. "You smell warm and sweet, Grace. I can't help but want to kiss you, but I wouldn't insult you for one minute."

"You haven't, Simon." Her face was rosy, warm from the pleasure of his kisses, and she could not help but smile at him. "I'm not fond of the idea of kissing, for I've met more than one man who felt it was his right to put his hands on me if I'd allowed him to walk me home after an event at church or if he'd spent an afternoon on my porch back home. But I find that you are different than most of the men I've known in the past, more genteel perhaps, a gentleman in your behavior. I don't feel that I must defend myself from you, for there is no fear of you in my mind."

Simon gently bent to place his lips against hers, his arms circling her waist as he held her a bit closer to himself. The kiss was brief, but he held her even after his lips lifted from hers. "You smell of flowers, Grace. Fresh and sweet."

She knew she was blushing, feeling flustered by his touch. "I'm going in the house now. I'm not certain that we've just held to the limit of friendship in the past few minutes, Simon. And I told Ethel I'd fix supper tonight. It's time to begin putting things together," she said, rising from the step beside him and walking across the porch.

Simon rose quickly, reaching ahead of her and opening the door for her to go into the kitchen. "And I'm going to take my horse back to the livery stable," he said, thinking of the gelding he'd tied to the front gate and then ignored until this minute.

Grace nodded quickly, her eyes shining in the late-afternoon sunlight. "You'd better hurry and take care of your horse, Simon. Get him settled in his stall with his supper."

He clapped his hat on his head and grinned at her. "I'll be back in a bit. Don't work too hard, ma'am."

Her smile was answer enough, he decided as he went around the corner of the parsonage and down the front walk to where his patient gelding awaited him.

He met two gentlemen from his congregation on his way back from the livery stable and made it his business to explain to them about his houseguest.

He was brief and to the point, assuring them that his housekeeper was keeping Grace company, and was met by their guarded approval. It seemed that they found it only fitting that a young woman whose life was in jeopardy should take shelter in their parsonage. With a clap on his shoulder, Simon found himself congratulated on his actions in defending her and offering her a temporary place to stay.

"Maybe the good Lord sent her to you, Reverend," one of them said with a sly grin. "It's about time for you to be taking a bride, ain't it?"

Simon laughed. "So my mother tells me. And perhaps she's right. I'll have to consider that Grace came to me at an opportune time in my life." With hearty farewells ringing in his ears, he made his way back to the parsonage. Bemused, yet made more confident by their attitude, he made haste to gain sight of his home, but met the sheriff before he'd gone far.

Lifting a hand in greeting, the lawman stopped him. "I'm going out for another try at picking up the Summers fella, Reverend. Sure hope I can get my hands on him this time, for I'm gonna feel a lot better once I slap him in a cell."

Simon breathed a sigh of relief as he walked to his back door and stood on the porch. Grace was busy at the stove and he watched her through the screen door for a few moments, caught by her movements in his kitchen. She was elegance personified, he decided, his gaze caught by her swishing skirts and the sound of her humming beneath her breath.

He opened the screen door and she turned quickly, her eyes lighting up as she smiled at him. "I'm making beef stew and dumplings for supper," she said, picking up two thick pot holders as she opened the oven door, her hand testing the degree of heat within before she closed it again.

She slid the Dutch oven from the back of the stove to a front burner and removed the lid, then picked up a bowl from the table. She scooped biscuit dough out of it by the spoonful, adding it to the bubbling gravy in the large pan before her, then replaced the lid atop the dumplings. A savory scent arose from the pan that drew Simon closer to her, and he inhaled deeply, signifying his approval of her work. Without hesitation, he bent to open the oven door, stepping back as she lifted the stew pot and settled it in the depths of the oven.

Grace stepped to the sink to wash her hands, then returned to the table, unconsciously lifting her hand to touch the swelling where hard knuckles had caught her cheekbone, for it had begun to throb when she bent low over the oven. A quick glance in Simon's direction made her rue the gesture, for he flinched, as if her pain were his own.

"He had no right to touch you, Grace."

"I know. But I still feel like I might have led him on in some way. I certainly didn't mean to, Simon, for I tried to ignore him as much as I could. Uncle Joe was pushing me to find a man and get married, and I suppose he thought Kenny was the one I should accept. Heaven knows the man made his intentions clear."

"Did he ask you to marry him?" Simon asked.

She laughed, a derisive sound. "In a roundabout way. He said I'd never get a better offer. That I was just a poor relation to Uncle Joe and he'd probably be glad to have me settled with a husband, so he wouldn't have to be responsible for me anymore."

Simon shook his head. "I doubt your uncle felt that way, Grace."

"Perhaps he did, Simon. He seemed to be pushing me at Kenny, even offered Kenny a small cabin on the ranch if I married him. I thought I was earning my keep, doing the cooking and my share of the chores, but perhaps it wasn't enough to please Uncle Joe."

"You did the cooking for his crew of men?" Simon asked.

"Yes, for Uncle Joe and six ranch hands. The housekeeper did the rest around the house, but once I arrived, Uncle Joe said I should cook. My mama made sure I knew my way around a kitchen by the time I was sixteen, so I managed pretty well."

"That was a lot of responsibility for a young woman, I'd say. I'd think your uncle would have kept you apart from his workers. He should have taken better care of you. Did he give you a wage for the work you did, Grace?"

Her eyes widened with surprise. "Why, no, of course not. He gave me a home and a room to call my own. I suspect he thought I owed him my work in return."

"Then how did you manage to buy clothing or anything else a woman might need?"

"I didn't. I just got along with what I had. And I don't want you to think I'm complaining, Simon, for I appreciated Uncle Joe. I just didn't feel he understood me very well."

"You need new clothing, Grace. I'm taking you to the general store to find a couple of dresses and anything else you need. You can consider your work here as my payment. And I won't take no for an answer. We're going now, in fact."

Even as he spoke, he hustled her to the front door, and with a nod at his housekeeper to take over the cooking, he escorted Grace down the walk and along the road to the general store. They found themselves the center of attention as they entered, with several of the town's ladies doing their shopping.

"Hello there, Reverend," one woman called out from the back of the store, to which Simon nodded and smiled, his hand on Grace's back as he led her to the wide walnut counter where the proprietor's wife awaited them.

"What can I get you, Reverend?" she asked, looking at Grace with interest.

Simon spoke simply and briefly. "This is Grace Benson, Joe Cumberland's niece. She's staying at the parsonage with myself and Mrs. Anderson, and she finds herself in need of some clothing. I fear she came to us unexpectedly and has a limited wardrobe. Can you take care of the situation, ma'am?"

"Why of course I can. Why don't you just go over and have a seat, maybe find part of the newspaper to read. It just arrived here an hour or so ago, so it's still in one piece. I'll just take care of Grace here."

She bent closer to Grace, her voice soft, as if she did not want to be overheard. "You just put yourself in my hands, dearie. We'll find you some dresses and all that goes with them. I'm sure you'll earn your way at the parsonage, helping out in the kitchen and especially in the garden. Young bones find it easier to kneel and pull weeds than older ladies can handle. Ethel Anderson is a good worker but I'm sure she can use your help."

She lifted several glass containers from the shelves behind her and held up garments for Grace's approval. "Here's a nice pink-checked dress, good enough for church on Sunday, or just to wear when you're on the porch swing of an evening."

She investigated the contents of another container and placed a petticoat on the counter, then two vests and two pair of drawers on top of it. "You can get along with but one petticoat, so long as you have vests and drawers to wear beneath it," she said nicely, shaking out the batiste fabric and showing Grace the lace that edged the neckline and shoulders.

"And here's another dress, more of an everyday thing to wear when you're in the kitchen or out in the garden," she said, holding up a darker print, green with daisies blooming across the skirt. "You'll still look nice, even when you're working."

"That's enough," Grace said quietly. "I don't want to run up a bill with you, for I only need some stockings and a pair of soft shoes for in the house. I have outdoor shoes and an old dress to wear in the garden."

"Well, then, let's just add one more thing. Here's a nice nightie, cotton, not too sheer, but sorta dainty-looking for a girl like you to sleep in." She held up a long gown, smocked across the bodice, and buttoned with small pearl fastenings down the front.

"This may be too much, ma'am," Grace said,

her eyes wide as she looked at the items on the counter.

And then from across the store, Simon called out politely. "Make sure she has enough to wear, and an extra pair of shoes, ma'am. You decide for her, for Grace won't spend money freely."

"I think we have it about solved, Reverend. Do you want to take a look at what we've chosen for her? I'll find a pair of house shoes to fit her now."

Simon shook his head as he approached the counter. "No, I'll trust your judgment. If you'll put this on my bill, we'll settle for it later."

Within moments she had found a pair of soft shoes for Grace to wear inside the house and added them to the rest of her choices. "That's fine, Reverend. I'll just bundle everything up for you." And within minutes, she'd done just that, sliding the package across the counter to Simon, who accepted it with a nod of thanks.

Simon took Grace's arm as they walked back to the parsonage. "Are you sure you got everything you need?" he asked.

She nodded, her throat filling with tears as she thought of his kindness. "You're a good man, Simon. Your mama must have raised you right," she said after a moment, and then was all too aware of the eyes that touched upon the two of them as they walked down the road. Her relief was great when they were once more inside the walls of the parsonage and she spent a happy half hour showing Ethel the clothing Simon had purchased for her.

"He did well," Ethel said finally. "You'll be able to go from one wash day to another without any trouble. Did you get some drawers?" she asked quietly as she looked over the pile of clothing.

Grace lifted the petticoat and showed Ethel the two pairs of drawers that had been included in the purchase. "I didn't need so much, but Simon insisted," she said ruefully.

"He did just right," Ethel said stoutly. "You needed every single thing you brought home with you."

"It didn't seem right to have a man buying clothing for me. It was sort of like he was responsible for me, Ethel. And I don't want him to feel that he is."

"He's taken on the job of looking after you, Grace. Let the man enjoy it."

"Enjoy it?" she asked, her eyebrows lifting.

"Exactly. The man is looking after you, just as he should. You're a guest in his home and he's sure enough planning on making your presence here a permanent thing, unless I'm missing my guess."

Simon came into the kitchen, causing Grace to wrap her clothing in a flurry of brown paper, lest he catch sight of the unmentionables she'd shown to

Ethel. Ignoring her flustered movements, he spoke quietly.

"I talked to the sheriff a few minutes ago, Grace. He came by and said he's on his way out to look for Kenny Summers again. When Judge Hale comes through on his regular schedule, the Summers fellow will face him if he can be found before then."

It was later that evening, supper dishes done and the kitchen cleaned, when Charlie showed up at the parsonage again, and his news was far from reassuring. It seemed that when he'd gone to pick up Kenny at Joe's ranch, the man was still nowhere to be found. A thorough search of the bunkhouse and barns came up empty, and the men who were questioned swore they had no knowledge of his whereabouts. He had disappeared and apparently without a trace.

"He must have fixed up his shoulder without help, Simon," the sheriff said quietly. "The doctor says he never came by to have him look at it."

Charlie was discouraged, angry and certainly not anxious to have Grace hear he'd come up empty-handed. He'd as much as said he would put Kenny in jail, and now he was in a position he dreaded.

Simon called to the kitchen for Grace to come into the parlor, and when she appeared in the doorway, Charlie rose to his feet. "Miss Benson." His greeting was quiet, his tone dark, and Grace sought Simon's gaze.

"What's wrong?" she asked, sensing that things were not as they should be.

"I fear I have disturbing news, ma'am," Charlie said quietly. "I couldn't find hide nor hair of Kenny Summers today. He seems to have found a hidey-hole and no one knows where it might be. I'm depending on Simon to look after you, Grace. Don't be going out on your own until we find the Summers fella."

Grace nodded her consent to his instructions and the sheriff took his leave, Simon seeing him to the door.

He came back to where Grace sat, her hands in her lap, her eyes bent downward to the floor, and with a deep sigh, he sat beside her, yearning to touch her, yet fearful of frightening the girl with the depth of his feelings. But lest she think he didn't care for her, that his words to her on the back porch didn't hold much water, he touched her cheek, bending to kiss her temple as he begged her to meet his gaze.

"Please, Grace. Look at me. I can't stand to see you so discouraged and sad." His hands were warm against her cold fingers and he drew them into his palms gently, lifting them carefully to his lips, where his mouth rested against her hands.

"Forgive me if I'm being too forward, Grace, but I want you to lean on me, to trust me. I see a definite problem, though, with you being here for so long a time. We don't have any choice about you staying, and I wouldn't have it otherwise. But I fear we may have to solve the dilemma rather quickly, lest there be a scandal involving your presence here. I think we need to consider marriage so that I can watch over you as a husband. It will resolve the situation…and give you the protection of my name."

She was silent and her hands formed fists within his palms. "Simon, I'm happy to be in your home. I wouldn't cause you any sort of problem with your congregation, not for the world. But marriage is a step I'm not really ready to consider right now. Ethel is kind to me and I'm safe here. I feel so comfortable with you and I trust you more than I can say. All of that means more to me than I can tell you. But I don't like to think of you offering yourself as a solution to my problems. I don't even know if I'd be a fit wife for a minister. I'm young and inexperienced and I don't know a whole lot about your work. And my experience with Kenny might not look good to the folks in the church."

"Grace, I don't like to be rushing you, but I don't think we have a lot of choice in the timing of this." He enclosed her hands tightly in his as he stood, tugging her to stand before him, one arm moving to circle her waist loosely. "You need to know that the kisses we've shared already mean we are well on our way to a formal betrothal, Grace. I think, under the circumstances, another kiss now will effectively seal our intentions."

Grace tilted her head back a bit, looking up into his eyes, feeling bewildered at his words, but willing to follow his lead in this. She felt a flush climb her cheeks again as his gaze touched upon her features, then dropped to where her dress clung to the lush lines of her breasts. He bent to her and his lips touched hers lightly, then as she returned the faint pressure of his kiss, he held her tighter, his other arm enclosing her in a firm embrace, clasping her closer to his broad chest.

His mouth was circumspect, his kiss not trespassing beyond her lips, and he lifted his head after long moments to meet her gaze once more. "You're a wonderful woman, Grace. Please say you'll be my bride. I can't tell you how much I'm looking forward to our marriage."

"All right, Simon, I'll marry you," she whispered.

From the kitchen came the sound of Ethel's voice calling her name, and Grace stepped back from him, her fingers spread wide against the rosy skin of her cheeks.

"I'm here in the parlor, ma'am. I'll be right out," she called in answer.

Simon followed her to the kitchen and Ethel smiled at them both. "I'm going to my room now. If you need me, just give a holler and I'll be right handy."

Simon spoke up. "I think Grace and I are going to sit out on the back porch for a while, Ethel. We've got some things to talk about, and perhaps we need to include you in the plans we're making."

"What are you plotting, Simon?" Ethel's arch gaze touched on Grace and then her smile widened to a grin as she returned her attention to Simon.

"I've been in the process of coaxing Grace to be my wife, Ethel. I've met with success and you're the first to know."

"Well, I'll be doggoned. Can't say I'm real surprised, but I'm sure pleased as punch. You know you're going to get tongues wagging, soon as the word gets out."

Simon laughed, drawing Grace close with the arm he'd wrapped around her waist. "They'll all be tickled to death, as will my family. The men on my church board have been steering me in this direction and my mother will think her dreams have come true."

"Don't know if I'll be able to sleep with all this going around in my head," Ethel said happily as she hugged Grace on her way out of the room.

"I think she approves," Grace said in a whisper, her blush radiant.

Simon opened the screen door and led her to the porch. "I wouldn't be a bit surprised," he told her. "Now, shall we take a walk through the apple trees out back?"

Chapter Four

"Could we stroll through the gate and down to the river?" Grace asked. "It's only a hundred feet or so and the moonlight should be pretty, shining on the water." She was much shorter than he, and her head tilted back as she looked up into his eyes. He caught up her hand again and placed it on his arm, then they turned together, walking slowly toward the apple orchard, where blossoms scented the air.

The grass was tall and the evening dew hung on each blade, but Grace was uncaring of damp shoes or hems. That she was walking with Simon in the moonlight was a joyous occasion, for she had all but agreed to his plan for her future.

They strolled together beneath the trees, both silent as though being together was enough to occupy their thoughts. The gate stood wide at the foot of the orchard and they passed through it, their steps taking them to where the stream flowed by on its way to the larger river outside of town.

Simon looked down at Grace, captured by the fragile line of her profile, certain he could make out a faint blush on her cheek as her fingers tightened a bit on his forearm. His words were soft, spoken near her ear as he bent to her.

"I've been thinking of you almost constantly today. In fact, almost since the first time I laid eyes on you," he said quietly, noting the quiver of her eyelashes as she shot a quick look in his direction.

"And what have you been thinking?"

"That I enjoy your company and looking at you. And now it seems I'm to spend my entire lifetime with you. I can't tell you how happy that makes me."

She halted and her hand lifted to touch her lips. "Simon, until now I hadn't thought of marriage in a positive way. Uncle Joe was so dead set on me settling down that I turned rebellious and was unwilling to consider it. But when you put it that way, that you're happy to spend your life with me, I feel like a woman who's been given a glorious gift. It all takes on a different light." And then she smiled at him, looking him full in the face.

"I've never had thoughts of a man in my life

before. Not like this, anyway. In fact, I'm embarrassed to admit how much..." She was silent then, as if she were unable to continue.

He felt an upwelling of emotion within him that was surprising, for he'd never ached for another woman as he did for Grace. His arms sought her lithe form and he held her close to him, carefully, as though he would not frighten her, and he dropped his head to leave a quick kiss upon her forehead. She caught her breath and shivered at the brush of his lips against her skin, then lifted her hands to his chest, her fingers clenching the fine cotton of his shirtfront.

It seemed to be enough encouragement for Simon, for he bent to her again. He was tall, his shoulders wide beneath the shirt he wore, his jacket fitting snugly across the wide lines of his back, and she felt suddenly very small before him, as though his greater size had made her own slender form more pronounced. *Feminine* was the word she thought of as she leaned into his body a bit, not wanting to be forward, yet needing to have the contact with him that had been tempting her for the past few minutes. Beneath her palm his heartbeat was solid, steady, if a bit hurried.

Simon touched her face with his fingertips, his hand cool against the flush of color she knew she wore. Tracing the line of her throat, he lifted his hand to her ear and his index finger touched the pulse that beat beneath it. It fluttered against his sensitive fingertip and she smiled, recognizing the rapid heartbeat as one that matched his own.

He hadn't thought to gain so much ground so rapidly with Grace, for he'd expected to spend weeks in taming her to his touch. And now she had responded to him quickly, assuring him that his attraction to her was not a one-sided affair.

"I don't mean to seem forward, Simon. I'm truly not in the habit of allowing men to hold me this way," she said quietly, her blue eyes fearless as she met his gaze. "I've been known to run the other way when the young men at home came too near in my earlier days."

He smiled down at her, the moonlight casting an unearthly glow upon her features, and he reveled in the open interest he saw in her expression. "I realize that you're not accustomed to being the recipient of a man's hands on you, Grace. I hope you know that I mean only respect and admiration when I touch you. Somehow I can't resist the need to hold you and kiss you, even though I feared you might be frightened by such intimacy."

"I'm not sure this is proper, our being so…" She glanced back over her shoulder toward the house, which was at a distance of perhaps a hundred feet or so. "Ethel will be pleased to know that we're having a wedding soon," she said.

Simon lifted his gaze and was not surprised to

see the kitchen curtains moving a bit, as though some hidden watcher had stepped back from the window. "She's an ideal chaperone for us. The ladies at church hold her in the highest regard. She's in charge of the ladies' society, you know. In fact, she'd like to pass the job along to someone else. She told me that she has enough to do, what with keeping the house up and tending to me. And now, she has another chick to look after."

"I won't cause her any work, Simon. I'm willing to do my share of the keeping of your house."

"I know you are, sweet. But Ethel won't be happy if she's not earning her pay."

He released his hold on Grace's waist and took her hand in his. They walked back from the stream, through the length of the orchard, speaking quietly of their lives, Simon telling her of his family, she speaking of her own parents and her life with them, then moving on to her uncle and the running of his house.

It was over half an hour later when they found themselves back at the porch and he drew her down again to the steps, his arm around her shoulders as if he would keep her from the chill of the late evening. They were quiet then, their thoughts perhaps on the same track, their hands touching, Simon leaned over to press his lips against her temple and then her cheek, before finally reaching to turn her face toward his, touching her mouth with his own, holding her against his chest. Her breasts were full and lush against him and his mind flew ahead to the nights when he would not leave her at a bedroom door, but instead share his bed with her.

"I think we'd better go in now," Grace said. "Ethel will be listening for us, I suspect."

Simon stood and drew her up beside himself. "I think you're probably right, Grace." He led her to the door and Grace took off her shoes, for they were damp from the dew. Then they went on through the kitchen to where a lamp awaited them in the hallway. He lifted it and in moments had escorted Grace to her bedroom door, opening it and stepping aside till she went into the room.

Ethel was in the kitchen before Grace arose in the morning, and when Simon entered the room close behind her, the housekeeper asked a quick question.

"Did you have a nice walk last night? I looked out when I came in the kitchen for a glass of water and saw you out in the orchard. And I saw your shoes by the back door, Grace. I'll bet they were wet with the dew, weren't they?" she asked, her gaze going from one to the other of them, bringing quick color to Grace's cheeks once more.

"The moonlight was beautiful, Ethel. You should have stepped outdoors and enjoyed it a bit. Our orchard is lovely this time of year, isn't it?" Simon asked, skillfully changing the subject, noting Grace's flustered state.

"We'll have quite a crop of apples if the bees are any indication," Ethel said, carrying a platter of bacon and eggs to the kitchen table.

"They didn't bother us any. They must have all been in the hive," Grace told her, recognizing that she wouldn't have noticed if they buzzed around her head, taken as she'd been with Simon's kisses and his warm embrace.

"I have a couple of calls to make this morning," Simon said, after asking the blessing on the food and passing the platter to Grace. He waited until Ethel had scooped two eggs onto her plate, then took the remaining three for his breakfast. There was toast and jelly to go with the eggs, and the bacon was fried crisply, just as he liked it. He ate leisurely, thinking of the day he'd planned, then spoke of his fears aloud to his housekeeper.

"I don't want Grace out of the house alone. The sheriff doesn't think it's a good idea for her to walk about town by herself. If you're going to the store, she might like to go along, but otherwise, she'll stick close to the house with you, Ethel."

"I understand the sheriff's fears. With that nasty fella running loose, it isn't safe for any young woman to be out on her own, I'd say."

"Well, I'll be back in a couple of hours. I'm only going just outside of town to where the Lashley family lives. The missus has been wanting to set a date for the new baby's christening, and I told Amos I'd drop by and see her for a few minutes. And then I'm going to stop at the Fletcher's farm and pay a call on the old gentleman. Mr. Fletcher's father," he said for Grace's benefit.

"I'll be safe here with Ethel," Grace assured him. She watched as he left the house, standing by the front window, her gaze taken by the straight line of his back, his graceful stride as he went out the gate, toward the livery stable where he would pick up his horse, or perhaps his buggy.

He'd left her with a heaviness in her breast, there where she had pressed herself just for a moment against his broad chest, a yearning in her heart for another touch of those warm lips against her skin, skating over her throat and mouth. He'd enjoyed their kisses last evening, she thought, for he'd left with a touch of arrogance, a jaunty tilt to his hat. And to her surprise, she'd enjoyed the touch of his lips on hers, the feel of his arms around her waist. It apparently depended on the identity of the gentleman when it came to kissing and hugging.

Simon was a man to be reckoned with once he got the bit in his teeth. He'd apparently decided to do some courting, and was heading full steam into his plans for the future. Pleased as she recalled his words, Grace hugged herself, remembering the time they'd spent under the apple trees last evening.

Preacher or not, he was a handsome fellow, with eyes that seemed to see into her soul. And wasn't that a fanciful thought?

Grace turned from the window, making her way back to the kitchen, meeting Ethel's knowing gaze as she crossed the floor to the pantry.

"You look pretty flustered," Ethel said with a grin that made her eyes light up with glee.

Grace sat down, her knees suddenly weak beneath her. "He's wonderful, Ethel. Like no one I've ever met, certainly a far cry from the men I've been acquainted with in the past. He has..." She hesitated for a long moment, as if the words she sought were just out of reach. "He has a way about him, a kindness you don't often see in a man, and he's a gentleman. I've known other men who didn't fit that description and seemed to be interested in me only because they thought I was pretty. That's not enough for me."

"It shouldn't be enough, and not just for you, but for any woman out looking over the current crop of men," Ethel retorted.

Grace felt her mouth tilt in a smile, one she could not have kept inside had she tried. "To answer your question, I think our friendship has become court-ship, and Simon is a determined man, Ethel. A wedding is the next step."

"I'm not surprised, child. Simon needs a wife, both as a man and a minister. And I'm not a bit surprised that he chose you to fill that place in his life." She held out her arms to Grace and held her close, patting her back and blinking back tears of joy.

"I'd like to cook for him tonight," Grace said, thinking of the ham in the pantry just crying for the oven. "Maybe I'll cut up some potatoes and onion and fix ham casserole."

Indeed, Simon was pleased at the dinner Grace put together, and he and his housekeeper exchanged a significant look over the steaming dish Grace carried to the table.

"Grace and I are having a good time together, Simon," Ethel said, serving herself once Simon had taken a share from the platter. She gave him an amused glance. "I'm glad you're planning on keeping her around."

"Best idea I've had in a month of Sundays," Simon replied, his eyes warm as he looked across the table at the young woman they were discussing. "Has she—"

"You betcha she has, and I've got a list already of what food we'll need for the reception, and some ideas about a dress for her," Ethel said, laughing at the look of bewilderment on Simon's face, as he recognized a woman with a plan.

"I'll leave it in your capable hands, then," Simon

told her. "I've wired my bishop, asking him to come here a week from Saturday."

He looked at Grace then and his smile was coaxing. "I want to let my parents know right away, so they can make plans to come for the wedding. Will you go with me to the telegraph office so we can send a wire?"

"You know I will, Simon. Just say the word," Grace told him, her heart racing as the whirlwind caught her up, for Simon was apparently a man who believed in moving right along.

"We'll walk to town tomorrow and then pick out a ring at the Emporium on the way home. All right?" he asked, grinning widely as though he was certain of Grace's compliance. And she could only nod, for her heart was too full to utter a word.

The man who approached the parsonage late the next afternoon was tall, a bit heavyset and past his prime. Simon watched him as he stepped onto the small porch, and, hidden behind the white lace curtains in the parlor, recognizing him from Grace's description.

"Looks like Grace's uncle has come calling," he said in an undertone as his housekeeper walked past the parlor. "Be sure that Grace stays in her room, please." The sharp knock on the front door was repeated before Ethel could reach it and Simon frowned at the caller's impatience. In moments the man was ushered into the parlor, and he stood just inside the doorway and gave Simon a cursory glance.

"You the minister?" he asked abruptly.

"I'm the Reverend Simon Grafton." His words of introduction were clear and precise as Simon faced the man. "And you are…perhaps Grace Benson's uncle?"

"That's me, young man. I heard word around town that you might know the whereabouts of my niece. Is that so?"

Simon nodded slowly. "Yes, as a matter of fact, I do."

Joe Cumberland looked impatient with the answer he obviously considered not to be information enough. "Well, where is she, Reverend?"

"To be very frank with you, sir, your niece would rather not be found right now. She took quite a beating from one of your ranch hands and she doesn't want to chance him finding her again. She's in a safe place for now."

"The man denies he hurt her. Foolish girl should have taken Kenny up on his proposal. He wanted to do the right thing and marry her and she was too uppity to accept him. About time she got married and had a family, if you ask me. She's well beyond the age of a girl getting settled."

"I've spoken about that very thing to your niece, sir, and I'm happy to tell you that she is about a week and a half from becoming my wife. The decision was made by the young lady, herself. I honestly don't think that a violent man such as Kenny is fit to be a husband for any young, gently reared woman. If you had seen Grace after that man assaulted her, you might have a different slant on things. The bottom line is this. I hope you'll accept Grace's decision to marry me. She fits my idea of a wife to be proud of, and I've vowed to take care of her and be a good husband to her."

"So far as Kenny's actions are concerned, it's his word against hers," Joe said harshly. "I've found Kenny to be a good worker and he's a bit impatient, I agree, but he means well, and Grace simply wasn't willing to listen to him. I came to ask her to come back to my ranch and settle down, and then spend some time with the man. Once he realizes she's come home, I'm sure he'll make a return, too. She might find him more to her liking if she gives him a chance. And she left me in the lurch, what with not having a cook, when she left so quick like. I think she needs to face her obligation to me and return to the ranch and live there. Give Kenny a chance to court her and get to know him. The man is intent on offering her marriage and I approve of him as a husband for her."

"We differ there, sir. She's not of that opinion, and with good reason. She's frightened of Kenny and unwilling to ever allow him near her again.

She's given me her pledge in answer to my proposal and I hope you'll accept that."

"Well, I'm the man responsible for the girl and I'm demanding you tell me where she is," Joe said, his hands clenched at his sides, as if he would welcome a physical confrontation.

Simon shook his head. "I'm sorry, sir, but I'm pledged to secrecy in this case. If and when Grace wants to return to your home, I'll bring her there to visit with you. But so long as you employ Kenny, I don't see that happening."

Joe's face turned red with anger. "I'll find out where you've stashed her, young man. And Kenny told me after you shot him that he was gonna file charges against you for assault. When Judge Hale comes to town, we'll see what he has to say about this."

"I'd like to see him file charges. And the sheriff would definitely like to see Kenny in the flesh. He'd slap him in a cell in no time. Charlie came to your ranch yesterday looking for Kenny and you said he wasn't to be found. The sheriff has seen Miss Benson and agrees that the physical violence visited upon her warrants a jail cell for Mr. Summers. You'd best turn him in instead of defending the man.

"I'll tell you now that Grace is under my protection, sir. You'll be happy to know that when Grace sought sanctuary here, she was given a free rein to make decisions about her future."

Joe turned and stomped from the parsonage, leaving Simon in the parlor, his housekeeper watching from the hallway.

"He's a harsh man, Pastor," Ethel said with a frown. "That young woman is better off where she is, I'd say."

"In our guest room?" Simon asked, his smile wide.

Ethel nodded. "Well, if the girl ever has a problem with him, we're of the same mind, I think. I'm more than willing to defend her. I'm a good one with that shotgun in the pantry and I'm a decent chaperone, I'd say. She'll be safe in this house."

"We'll manage to guarantee that, but we need to keep the law in the picture. I wouldn't be surprised if Sheriff Wilson didn't see Grace's uncle here, but if not, I need to let him know," Simon told her.

His visit with the sheriff would be short, Simon decided as he walked quickly down the street to where the jailhouse sat, across from the hotel. The door was open, the day being a fine one, and Charlie Wilson stood just inside. He nodded at Simon and waved at the chair, a tacit invitation for the visitor to sit down.

Simon shook his head. "I'll only be a moment. Just wanted you to know I just had a visit from Grace Benson's uncle. He was most adamant about finding his niece and taking her home with him. I told him Grace and I were planning a wedding and the Summers fellow was completely out of the picture."

"I'd say congratulations are in order, Simon," the sheriff said with a grin. "You're getting a fine young lady. Just don't let that girl out of your sight, Preacher. I was about to take a walk over to see you. There's trouble in town. One of the ladies over at the saloon had a run-in with a man. The bartender was here and told me Belle's pretty well beat up and bloody. Seems one of her customers got pretty rough with her."

"Do they have any idea who the man was, Charlie?" Simon asked.

"I'm going to speak with her when she's able and find out what she knows," the lawman answered. "I'll let you know what I hear, but the bartender said the fella was a regular customer."

"Perhaps I should stop by and see her later on," Simon offered. "If it should turn out to be the Summers fella, it'll be another strike against him."

"That's for certain," the sheriff agreed, standing and offering his hand to Simon as the younger man clapped his hat on his head and went out the door.

Chapter Five

Simon went into the house, his gaze sweeping the parlor as he stood in the wide doorway, his eyes focused on Grace. "I've heard some bad news," he said, knowing that his face was somber. He didn't have it in his heart to try for a cheerful demeanor.

Grace lost her smile as he spoke and a shiver traveled through her. "I think I may already know what the problem is, Simon."

Ethel came into the parlor as Grace spoke. "Have you heard the news, Simon? Our neighbor ran in for a minute this afternoon and told us one of the women over at the saloon has been attacked and hurt pretty bad. Did the sheriff tell you about it?"

Simon nodded. "I heard it from Charlie Wilson.

He told me he's on the lookout for the man, and I'm sure you can guess who his prime suspect is. He's going to talk to Belle and the bartender and see if they are willing to identify the fella."

He turned to Grace then. "Let's go for a walk, sweetheart. I need to talk to you." Grace nodded, and followed him out the door into the backyard. The sun was nearing the horizon, the sky fading into the colors of twilight.

They walked slowly into the orchard, where the blossoms had been falling to the ground, the spring breeze blowing them from the trees all day long. It was like a fairyland with the grass barely peeking through the pale blossoms, the scent of springtime surrounding them. They walked to the end of the stand of trees, to where the fence enclosed the lush grasses of the field, where only a narrow path led to the stream behind the house.

"I've been talking to the sheriff, Grace. I'm worried about your safety, so long as there's a madman on the loose." He turned her to face him and held her in a loose embrace, aware of her body trembling against his. "When the sheriff told me about the attack on Belle over at the saloon I could only be thankful that it wasn't you who'd been so terribly used."

Grace leaned against him, relishing the solid feel of him, the warmth of his embrace. She felt driven to confide in him, to be honest about the experiences in her past, when she was younger and her parents were still alive, even though he might look askance at her. Her words were slow, almost a whisper as she began.

"Simon, I fear that here, inside me, I'm not a gentlewoman, such as would make a good wife for you. For there were times in my past, when I was but a young girl, barely out of pinafores and aprons, when I found myself a target for several of the young men in our town. They told me I was pretty, and I knew their eyes spent a lot of time looking me over sometimes. It made me feel self-conscious, as if I'd dressed in such a way as to invite their attentions. And I hadn't, Simon. I swear to you I was modest and tried my best to act as a lady should. But apparently some of the older fellows thought their liking me was reason enough to deserve my company. I found myself many times going home early from the Grange or a church social, because I feared the attentions of the young men. I must have somehow made them think I was available for their nonsense, for they pestered me, trying to…"

Simon shook his head, holding her before him, the better to speak his thoughts, and his smile was gentle as he looked down at the fragile beauty in his arms. "I almost sympathize with them, Grace. You have a lovely face and form. You're the most appealing woman I've ever known. That the young men chased after you doesn't make you less than you are. The poor lads no doubt spent sleepless nights dreaming of you, for you are a beautiful woman, and they were only human."

He drew in a breath and his arms tightened around her, holding her firmly against his body, her hips pressed to his, her soft breasts cushioned against his firm chest.

"Perhaps I'm of the same sort, but I've never meant to insult you with my advances, Grace, for I wouldn't do anything to cause you to fear me. Yet, I can understand how the young men of your community felt. There is about you a loveliness that would draw any man to you."

She tilted her head back and met his gaze, her eyes blurred with the tears that would not be halted. "Thank you for your words, Simon. But again, I'm fearful of being less than the woman you think dwells within the shell you see before you. I'm not feeling like much of a lady right now for I've been wishing for your arms to hold me, Simon. I think about you so much, when I go to sleep at night and when I wake up in the morning. In fact, it seems that you're in my mind all day—"

"You're such an innocent, Grace. I doubt you have any idea how badly I want you and how I'm counting the hours until our wedding. I'd thought to take it slowly and spend weeks in walking by your side, talking of my prospects and finding out more about you. Instead I've talked you into a wedding and used my fears for your well-being to coax you into my plans. I want to spend all the hours of the day with you, Grace. I can't wait to make you my wife. Your uncle was here and I told him of our plans. He didn't like it. If I didn't feel I have to let my parents know, I fear I'd rush you to my church's headquarters and have the bishop perform a ceremony posthaste. I want this wedding more than you can imagine."

Grace frowned at his words. "I wouldn't really mind that, Simon, but I fear your mother and father might want you to marry someone they know. Perhaps a girl from your hometown. Someone they've thought of as a perfect wife for you."

He laughed, swinging her from her feet. "No, they'll be pleased that I've found you, for my mother has been after me for months, telling me it was time to marry and begin a family of my own. And I know they'll love you and think you a perfect choice." His eyes sparkled as he set her back down, holding her until she caught her balance. And then he sobered suddenly, his heart aching as he saw tears on her cheeks.

"You're crying, Grace." His fingers lifted to her face and he wiped away the evidence of dampness that lingered there.

She swallowed her sobs, her words muffled against his shirtfront. "I want so badly to be the right woman for you. I don't know if I can act and speak and dress as a minister's wife should. I have no idea how to be what you need for I can only be as I am. And as for my tears, they are but tears of joy, Simon," she whispered. Her heart was so full, it felt as if it might burst within her, and she wrapped her arms around his waist and held him tightly. "I didn't know that I could feel this way about a man. I've never known anyone like you, and never has any man made me yearn for his touch as you do. What if your bishop doesn't approve of me? What if he doesn't think I'm good enough to fill the position of wife to you?"

"Don't think that for a minute, sweetheart. He'll think you're a fine, upright girl, a real addition to my parsonage." His arms tightened around her and his kisses warmed her until she pressed herself against his muscular form.

Simon was tempted mightily. His breathing was harsh, his need for her almost more than he could keep under control. She was slender, yet her body was lush and ripe, and he inhaled deeply, his mind filled with her scent, the aroma of flowers and the soap she'd used. The reins of his control threatened to slide from his grasp but he would not, could not do as he yearned. For the privileges he craved were not his to claim just yet. He trembled with the desire to possess the girl he held in his arms and struggled with the cravings of his body.

The sun had gone down and twilight settled around them as they walked back toward the house. Simon led her up the path and onto the porch where he opened the door, ushering her into the kitchen. The lamp was turned down low and he lifted the globe to blow it out before they walked down the hallway to the parlor. It, too, was empty, for it was apparent that Ethel had gone to her room.

"I think we were wise to come inside, Grace. I wanted to be in the house before night fell."

He lit the small lamp on the parlor table, then carrying it in one hand, led her to her room, holding the door open until she lit her candle. She turned and walked back to where he stood in the doorway. Her hands reached for him, settling on his shoulders, and he looked down at her with a warmth she could almost feel, so warm and tender were his eyes, so happy the smile he wore. She lifted on tiptoe and kissed his cheek, only to be halted by the hand that was not holding the lamp.

"You won't get away so easily, sweetheart," he said, bending to press his lips against hers, his free arm circling her waist. His lips were firm, his need apparent, as he felt his heartbeat thunder in his chest. She was soft against him, and he ached to touch her, to caress her and taste the sweetness of her skin. But it was not to be, here in the doorway of her bedroom, with Ethel in the house. Reining in his desire, he released her from his hold and she stepped back, seemingly reluctant to end the kiss he'd instigated.

But he gritted his teeth and bowed his head. "I'll see you in the morning. I'll be up early and put wood in the cookstove for you." His head lifted, his eyes touched her face, seeming to capture her very essence as he examined each feature. "Good night, Grace."

"Good night," she answered, wondering how it would be when she went with him into his bedroom each night and they slept together on that wide bed. And for her thoughts felt a hot flush rise to her cheeks. Almost as if he knew the images that flitted through her mind, he leaned closer and his words were a temptation in her ear.

"It won't be long now. Just another week." His hand touched her shoulder and brushed across the fullness of her breast as he turned from her. And for that he would not apologize, he decided firmly. It was the least bit of comfort he could gain from this encounter, and he would cherish the scant second of warmth he'd felt as his fingers touched the rise of her bosom.

Grace stiffened and stepped back from him, her face crimson.

"Grace, we're going to be married. Surely I can be forgiven for an innocent touch." Simon looked down at her, watching her as she blushed all the more and ducked her head before she managed a reply.

"After we're married, I suppose it won't be an issue. But right now, I'm not ready to accept—"

"You have my apology, then, sweetheart. I wouldn't cause you embarrassment for anything in the world."

"I can't help how I feel, but I don't mean to make a fuss over it. I'll walk down the aisle to you whenever you say, Simon."

"That's what I wanted to hear."

Charlie Wilson stood at the doorway of the parsonage the next morning, nodding politely as Simon opened the door for him. "How are things going?" he asked, extending a hand to the young man.

Simon greeted him, then motioned to the parlor doorway. "Won't you come in, sir?" he invited, aware of Grace behind him in the hallway. Without hesitation, the lawman stepped into the parlor and took a seat, Simon following behind him with Grace in tow. He settled on the sofa with her at his side and waited patiently for Charlie to state his business. It didn't take long, for the lawman cleared his throat and began.

"I wanted to be certain of where we stand, Miss Grace. You have no intention of returning to your uncle's ranch, have you?"

Grace shook her head. "Certainly not, sir. Simon has asked me to marry him, and Mrs. Anderson is making lists and plans for the reception. Even if all of that were not so, I'd never go back there so long as Kenny is on the loose. I feel much safer being in town."

Charlie looked quickly at Grace. "I'm here on a mission. Surely Simon has told you about Miss Belle over at the saloon being hurt. Well, the doctor stopped by to tell me he'd been by to visit her again.

"Belle told the doc who the fella was and soon as I get a posse together, I'll be after him again. I'm sure hoping with a dozen men combing that part of the area, by this time tomorrow afternoon, he's gonna be in jail."

"Who did it? A stranger? Or one of the ranch…" Grace's words trailed off as Charlie Wilson shook his head. "It was Kenny Summers, wasn't it?" she asked, feeling the blood drain from her head, fearing the worst. "Is the woman badly hurt?"

"She's alive. Pretty well stove up, couple of broken ribs and a pile of bruises. But she can talk and she identified Kenny. Told the doctor what he was wearing and described the bandage on his shoulder left over from when you shot him, Simon. And a birthmark he's got on his—" The sheriff cleared his throat loudly. "Anyways, she smacked him on his wounded shoulder and made him madder than a hornet. Probably shouldn't have done it, but she was fighting like the dickens, from what she said.

"Anyway, she identified him to the satisfaction of the law. I've got Judge Hale heading this way by the end of next week. If all goes well and if Summers is finally located, he'll no doubt be hauled off to a Federal facility. He's proved to be a slippery fella so far. I'm gonna feel kinda foolish if we can't lay hands on him before the judge shows up. The young women in this town shouldn't have to fear walking out alone or wondering if the fellas they're with are out for more than a few kisses," Charlie said.

Simon rose. "Let me know what you find, Sheriff. I have to make a couple of calls on sick folks this morning. I don't want to be gone too long for I hesitate to leave the parsonage for any length of time."

Charlie stood and followed Simon to the doorway. "Just be careful that no one follows you, Reverend. Keep a good eye out." The sheriff looked fierce as he touched a hand to his gun, removing it from its holster, checking to be sure it was fully loaded. "Everyone in the area knows that Kenny is a wanted man, and if I find out that Joe Cumberland is keeping him hidden from me, there'll be hell to pay. I'll guarantee you that."

* * *

Simon and Grace sat in the parlor after supper, both of them excited about their future together, neither of them wanting to move apart, so enraptured were they with each other. Simon leaned closer for a moment, his need for her holding him in thrall, for he could think of nothing but the wedding to come and the plans yet to be confirmed.

"I must send a wire to my parents, Grace. I'd thought to write, but I can't wait so long for them to know about you. I hope you haven't any doubts about the date I've set for our wedding."

"I'm agreeable to Saturday next, Simon. When will you wire your parents?"

"Right away. I want them to have plenty of time to make plans."

"I'll leave it up to you to make the arrangements. I'll meet you at the altar as soon as you ask your bishop about speaking the marriage vows for us."

"I've notified all of my deacons that there is to be a wedding on Saturday next. Most all of them already knew of your presence in my home, but I wanted to make it apparent to all the men that there will be a wedding right soon. I don't want any gossip about you being here. Ethel, bless her heart, is a fine chaperone but I think my church board is relieved to see the problem solved so readily." He rose then and drew her to her feet.

"Come with me to the rail station. I want to send a wire and I don't want you out of my sight for a minute." He tilted her chin upward and his mouth found hers again, his lips firm as he claimed hers, and then he grasped her hand, leading her to the hallway, where he called out to his housekeeper, who was in the kitchen.

"Ethel, we're going to the rail station to send a wire to my parents. We won't be long."

The older woman came from the kitchen, her face alight with a wide smile. "We'll have a real celebration in no time, Simon. I've been making out a menu and I'm going to talk to the ladies at church about helping out with the food for the reception." She made a shooing motion with her hands. "The pair of you go on now and take care of your plans."

When Simon and Grace arrived in town to send the wire, the stationmaster watched the young preacher and the lovely woman by his side, perhaps recognizing that something of great import was happening right here in the telegraph office. For Simon's hand trembled as he wrote the words that would be delivered to his parents' home in Oklahoma the next morning.

"I've found my bride. Come immediately. Wedding on Saturday next."

And then he sent a few terse words to his bishop, reaffirming his request for that man's presence to officiate at his wedding to Miss Grace Benson.

Chapter Six

It was the next day just after noontime when the lone gunman rode along the riverbank and hid within the thick stand of trees. As though he thought himself a smaller target, less visible to those he watched, Kenny Summers dismounted from his horse and tied the animal to a tree limb lest he follow where he should not go. Hiding amidst the trees was an easy task, for the heavily wooded area gave him shelter and he had a good view of the house, the parsonage wherein lived the man he sought.

The preacher had not seen him, even though he'd been following him for a long distance this morning. He could have fired then, but it was more important to find out where he'd stashed Grace Benson than to kill the preacher man right away.

And before him now, through the window near
the back porch, he caught sight of the woman he
sought. Grace Benson was in his sights and his
anger at her grew by leaps and bounds. She had
no right to be living with the preacher. She'd been
offered marriage by Kenny, and she'd turned him
down. The urge to lay his hands on her swelled
within the man and his hands shook as he held
his gun. It would serve her right if he took aim at
her through the window. But for now, he decided a
warning would do. Would suit his purpose better.

He'd watched as the older woman came out and
had hung what looked like dish towels on a line on
the back porch, then gone back in the house. Maybe
he'd take aim, next time she walked out the door.
That would get Grace Benson's attention. She'd
know then he meant business. For surely she'd have
a good idea who'd fired the gun.

He saw the female move from the window then.
Grace Benson for sure, for the housekeeper was
taller, a larger target. He could have picked her off
like an empty can on a fence post had he wanted to,
earlier. Maybe just a shoulder shot would put her
out of commission, leaving Grace more vulnerable
to him.

And having Grace in his power was the final
victory he sought. His body craved the womanly
shape, her curving form, and his greedy soul
sought out her inheritance. For he'd overheard Joe

Cumberland speak of it one day, and vowed he'd claim it the day he married the girl.

He'd almost had her, almost won her as his bride, for even her uncle had approved of him. But the preacher had snatched her away. Bringing her home with him, like a dog with a bone. It had been a good trick to pull, for it had taken Kenny a while to figure out where she was stashed. Until he'd followed the preacher man back to the parsonage and caught sight of Grace there.

And so he watched the place where his target hid. Perhaps she'd come out and he could lure her far enough from the house to make her an easy pickup. His horse could run faster than a slip of a girl, and once she was away from shelter, he'd get her.

For now, though, he concentrated on the woman, the old lady who kept a tight rein on Grace. She wouldn't be any great loss to anyone, maybe to the preacher man, but he'd already made Kenny angry enough to get rid of him, too. Right now, he was ready to shoot the first one of them who came through that back door. Not Grace, he corrected himself quickly, but if the old woman was laid up with a bullet wound the girl would have to come out of the house sometime, maybe to tend the garden, at least show herself on the porch.

The trees hid him as Kenny moved to another spot, one in which the house was more clearly visible through the trees. And there he waited. And felt a surge of triumph when the old lady opened the back door and came out on the porch, a rug in her hand. She stood on the end of the small porch and shook the rug a bit, looked down at it and lifted it to shake it again.

The gunman raised his rifle, a weapon he'd practiced with until it felt a part of his body. It rested on his shoulder, and he winced at the pressure from it, for his wound was still giving him problems. But he forgot all of that as he took aim and his finger tightened on the trigger. As the old woman stood, rug in hand, he pulled back his index finger and the shot was fired.

The bullet missed the target he'd aimed for, hitting instead the siding of the house behind her. She'd bent just a bit as he shot and his aim had been off. And then she slumped to the floor, fainting dead away.

The sound of the rifle bullet being fired brought Grace out the door, and the sight of Ethel lying on the porch made Grace fall to her knees, behind the railing, visible between the upright spokes. He heard her voice call out.

"Ethel. Oh, Ethel." She bent low, her attention only for the woman before her. Her hands touched Ethel with care, as if she sought out any sign of blood or injury, but she seemed to find nothing untoward, only a woman who seemed to be regaining consciousness, her eyes blinking a bit, her voice speaking Grace's name.

Grace was in his sights, but Kenny lowered his gun, for she was not the target yet. He'd get to her. He crept backward from his hiding place, untied his horse and was on his way, confident that Grace would be more readily available to him, with her guardian warned to stay clear. He'd return, with provisions enough to take up a watch for hours.

Grace bent over Ethel, her hands careful as she brushed back the woman's hair, leaning over her as she blinked and looked up, fright alive on her face as she thought of Simon next door in his office at the church.

She cried out to Simon, calling him urgently as she heard him enter the house, banging on the wooden siding near her. Within seconds, he was there, kneeling by her side, and Grace cast him a look of fear.

"Someone tried to hurt her, Simon. I'm so glad he missed his target."

"I heard the sound of a gun from my office and came home as quickly as I could, Grace." He looked up at the side of the house, where Ethel had been standing only moments before. "There's where the bullet went into the siding," he said, pointing to the hole over their heads.

"What shall I do?" Grace asked. "I can run to

find the doctor if you want me to. Or else stay here with Ethel while you go. Perhaps he should take a look at her. I think she's only frightened, but I'd feel better if he saw her."

"I'll carry Ethel into the kitchen, Grace. And then you shut the back door and lock it." He lifted the woman into his arms and carried her over the threshold into the kitchen, placing her on the floor there, Grace bending over her. "I'll go for the doctor and you stay right here on the floor with Ethel. I'm going to get the shotgun for you, and if you see anyone trying to open the door or see a gun out there, don't be afraid to shoot. I'll hurry and be back as soon as I can. Just fire that gun if you think you should. Don't take any chances," he said quickly.

"I won't. I'll be all right here," she told him, grasping the gun he handed her and placing it on the floor by her side. She bent low, whispering Ethel's name as the woman slowly regained her awareness.

Grace dampened one of the dish towels beneath the pump and washed Ethel's face, then a movement from the woman caught Grace's quick attention and she bent low to hear the words Ethel spoke.

"I think someone shot at me, Grace," she whispered.

"Simon has gone for the doctor, Ethel," Grace

said quietly, her eyes wet with tears she'd shed as she'd tended her friend.

"Now, blow your nose and don't be fussing so," Ethel managed to whisper. "I'll be fine. There's no need for Doc to come here. I haven't been shot, have I?" She lifted her head and looked down at her body, clucking her tongue. "Seems to me I'm in good shape, girlie."

"If I had whoever shot you at you in my sights, I'd pepper him good," Grace said.

Ethel's voice was weak, but anger gave her words emphasis. "I'll bet dollars to doughnuts it was that Kenny Summers. He's found out where you are, Grace." She leaned on one elbow and lifted herself from the floor. "Give me a hand here, Grace. Help me sit up." Together they leaned against the wall near the stove, Grace with an arm around Ethel's shoulders and holding her hand while they waited.

The front door opened and Simon's voice called out. "It's only me, Grace. I've found the doctor and he's with me."

Grace felt a surge of relief such as she'd never known before, sitting there on the kitchen floor, helping to hold Ethel erect. Her hands trembled as she looked to the hallway door and watched Simon enter. His gaze touched her face immediately and his smile, though strained, was welcome.

"Are you doing all right?" he asked, looking at Ethel, who was pale but unhurt.

She nodded, and the doctor came quickly to kneel by her side. He moved her a bit, freeing her from Grace's hold, and Ethel groaned, her eyes closing tightly as he settled her on the floor before him.

"I'll get a pillow for her head," Grace said and ran to the parlor where the decorative pillows she'd made just a few days since were perched on the sofa. Carrying one back to the kitchen, she slid it beneath Ethel's head and then grasped that lady's hand again.

"I'm fine, Doc. Just feeling kinda woozy from all the excitement, I think. The damn fool missed me, hit the side of the house instead," Ethel said in a low whisper.

"You just lie still for a few minutes, ma'am," the doctor said, his hands steady as he lifted Ethel's hand to take her pulse.

"It looks to me like you did a fine job here, taking care of Mrs. Anderson, young lady," the doctor told Grace. He found a bottle in his seemingly bottomless satchel and opened it, shaking four pills out into his palm. "Just give her one of these now, and then another in three or four hours. She'll be just fine after a good night's sleep. Takes more than a nasty scare to get a good woman down," he said with a chuckle, closing his bag and rising from his knees to stand by Simon.

"I'll stop by tomorrow to make sure you're feeling up to snuff, ma'am," he said to Ethel, watching as she swallowed the pill. "But I don't think we've got anything to worry about."

"I'll take good care of her, sir," Grace assured the medical man. "I'll make her some soup and a pot of tea so she'll have something nourishing when she gets hungry. And I'll put her on the sofa in the parlor to rest."

The doctor smiled at her. "You'll do, girl. I won't worry a bit about my patient while you're here."

"Well, Grace isn't going anywhere, sir," Simon said, his gaze touching on Grace's flushed face and slender form. "Between the two of us, we'll look after Ethel."

The doctor nodded his agreement with Simon's plan and then made another suggestion. "You'd better see the sheriff right off, Reverend. He needs to know what's going on here. He'll no doubt want to go out back and see if there's any sign of a gunman out there."

"I'll walk over there right away, sir. Shouldn't be gone more than five minutes or so. Grace will hold the fort while I'm gone."

"We'll be fine. I think maybe Ethel will sleep for a while. She looks kinda drowsy to me," Grace said. She helped Ethel to her feet and headed for the hallway, the sofa in the parlor her goal.

"That pill was pretty powerful. Should help her sleep for at least three hours, maybe longer," the doctor said. "It'll give you time to make that soup," he told Grace with a wide grin. He turned then and, satchel in hand, went out the front door, followed by Simon.

When Simon reported the latest incident to Charlie Wilson, he was indeed upset over the latest shenanigans, as he put it, to be going on in his town. He followed Simon from the jailhouse and went with him back to the parsonage. Leaving Simon in the house, Charlie went out beyond the garden where he found evidence of a horse having been tied to a tree near the riverbank. The grass was stomped down there, as if someone had walked back and forth, and the parsonage's back porch was clearly visible from the site. Although protected by a thick stand of trees, the gunman had found an ideal spot to hide while he did his dirty work.

Charlie went up to the house, knocking on the back door, till Simon unlocked it and welcomed him into the kitchen. The door had rarely been locked and the key had a difficult time turning in the chamber.

"I'll need to oil that a bit, make sure it works well from now on," Simon said. It was not the general practice for anyone in town to lock their houses, but Simon vowed he'd make certain they were behind locked doors from now on, as he told the sheriff.

The night was long, for Grace refused to leave the bedchamber where Ethel slept. She dragged in a chair from her own room and sat on it throughout the midnight hours. At four in the morning, when the sky had begun to turn an unearthly shade of gray, Simon put his foot down.

"You're going to bed, Grace. If I have to put you there, I will, but it isn't doing you a bit of good to sit here all night, when Ethel is sleeping like a rock. She's not due for another pill till 6:00 a.m. and I can sit here until then and give it to her. But you are going to bed. Right now."

And so stern was his voice, so dark the eyes that bade her obey, Grace went to her bed. She'd but dozed through the night hours, and almost fallen from the chair she sat in more than once. Her bed looked mighty welcoming, she decided, donning her nightgown and crawling beneath the covers. She slept immediately, and it was almost ten o'clock, midmorning, before she awoke to find Simon standing beside her bed.

"My word, I've slept too long. I wanted to make breakfast for Ethel and here it's long past time for her bowl of oatmeal."

Simon smiled smugly. "I took care of breakfast. She turned thumbs-down on oatmeal, by the way. Said that tea and toast sounded good. So I made them both and carried up a tray. And did it quietly so you'd sleep a bit longer."

"Well, I'm getting up now. I'll put some chicken on to cook in the big kettle and make her some soup for dinner. She seemed to enjoy the vegetable soup I made yesterday. Shouldn't take too long if you'll get out of here and let me wash up and get dressed."

Simon laughed as he offered a parody of a bow in her direction. "Yes, ma'am. Whatever you say, ma'am. I've been thinking I should do my studying and so on right here instead of leaving you here alone. I'm going to get my books and bring them back and make myself a place to work in the parlor. Will you mind having me around?"

"Of course not," Grace said. "In fact, I think I'll enjoy having you in the house."

"I'd say that settles that, then," Simon told her, and with a final grin in her direction, he walked from her bedroom and closed the door behind himself.

In less than fifteen minutes he appeared at the back door, his arms loaded with papers and books. Grace unlocked the door and let him in, following him to the parlor where he cleared off the library table and set up a temporary office, his pens and inkwell sitting on a fresh desk blotter, his books and writing materials stacked neatly.

She left him to his work and returned to the kitchen where she set about the soup-making process. By the time steam had begun to rise from the big kettle, Simon was back, rubbing his hands together, a wide smile on his face.

"Isn't that soup done yet?" he asked, inviting a laugh from Grace.

"Not yet," she said. "I'm a decent enough cook, but I don't work magic."

He laughed and stole a quick kiss and a longer embrace. "I sure do like you, Miss Grace," he said with a lifted eyebrow. "You smell just like a woman should."

"And how is that?" she asked, turning back to the stove where she'd been adding cut-up potatoes and carrots to the soup.

"Oh, sort of like chicken and some onion cooking in a kettle on the stove, with a bit of lilac soap smelling like spring, right there on your pretty throat, and an added smitch of just pure woman."

Grace blushed prettily, her eyes warming with laughter as she tossed him a teasing look over her shoulder. "And how does pure woman smell, Reverend?"

He frowned. "Reverend, huh? You didn't have to remind me that I'm supposed to be stern and upright and all solemn-faced, ma'am. Now I'm bound to act like a dignified gentleman when I tell you that there's nothing in the world that has the sweet aroma of a woman. And having you in my kitchen makes me think I'm halfway to heaven."

"Just behave yourself, Simon. You're making me blush and simper like a ninny. And I don't like that."

He stepped closer to peek over her shoulder, his whisper soft in her ear. "I like it when you blush, sweetheart, and you are the furthest from a simpering ninny of any female I've ever seen. You're a lady, through and through, and a lovely addition to my home.

"Now," he asked in a tone that struggled to be proper and solemn, "when do you suppose that soup will be fit to eat?"

She poked a bit of carrot experimentally. "Not long. About enough time for you to find some bowls to put it in and a knife to spread butter and jam on the bread with. Shortly after that, we'll have soup. I've got coffee made up fresh or there's milk to drink if you'd rather."

She turned to the kitchen dresser and quickly sliced off half a dozen thick pieces of a fresh loaf of bread, transferred them to a small plate and covered it with a napkin to keep it fresh. "Once you escort Ethel from her room we can gather around and dish up," she told him, stepping back to check out the soup a last time.

"I fear that once she comes out here and eats some solid food she'll be hunting up her apron again."

Simon watched her, his gaze warm as he noted every movement of her hands, each bend of her body, the swish of her skirts as she readied her meal, and his heart leaped within his chest as he cherished the look of her, the purely feminine being that was Grace.

Then, within moments, sniffing with appreciation at the scent of food, Ethel appeared at the kitchen door without prompting. "I'll just wash up a bit and then sit down with you at the table," she said, heading for the sink where soap and water awaited her. "Looks almost ready to me," she said with a smile.

Simon came in and took his seat, waiting for the two women to join him. "You can both go right ahead and eat. The food is all blessed. I included yours when I prayed over mine."

Grace looked up at him and laughed aloud. "Impatient, are you?"

"Just a little, ma'am. Wait till you taste this soup, Ethel. My new cook is a talented lady."

Later in the afternoon, Charlie came back to the parsonage. Simon met him at the door, opening it wide to allow his entry. "What's going on?" he asked, noting the rifle Charlie carried.

Charlie shook his head. "Still no news. I'm feeling like the man has pulled the wool over our eyes, me and Grace's uncle both. I honestly don't think he knows where Kenny got to, for he sure seemed on the up-and-up when I went out to talk to him today. He said he's got all of his men on the lookout for him, but they'd come up dry."

"Well, I think he was in my backyard yesterday," Simon said harshly.

"I know. And I want to take another look around out there. That's why I'm here, Simon." He looked around himself then and spoke more quietly. "Where is Grace? I sure hope she's here in the house with you."

"She is, Charlie. Out in the kitchen, as a matter of fact." Simon led the way through the house to where Grace stood at the kitchen table, rolling out a piecrust.

"Hello there, Sheriff. You should have put your visit off for an hour or so and I'd have had this pie baked."

"Oh, I could manage that, ma'am. I'll just take my little walk by the riverbank and then come back to see how it's coming along."

His grin seemed to put her at ease. "Will you stay for supper, Charlie?" she asked, following him to the back door.

"You bet," he said quickly, tipping his hat brim a bit as he turned, heading for the back of the lot, making his way toward the riverbank. He'd gone perhaps two hundred feet when he looked down at the ground, bending to one knee to brush at something. He picked up the object and looked toward the house.

"I'm going out there," Simon said, obviously interested in whatever it was that had drawn the lawman's interest there along the path by the stream. Perhaps he'd caught sight of hoofprints or even those of a man, he decided.

Charlie turned back then, retracing his steps through the garden, waiting for Simon. "Look here what I found," he said, his hand holding a bullet casing.

"I don't know why I didn't find this yesterday, but it doesn't matter now. I caught sight of a set of boot prints leading to where he tied his horse. Probably took his shot and then vamoosed quick as he could."

"I wonder how long he'd been watching the house," Simon mused.

"We'll probably never know. For that matter he could be out beyond the stream even now. The trees are pretty thick out there. I'd suggest you keep your womenfolk away from the window and the back door, son."

"I'll do that. You know, I'm dead certain we're looking for the Summers fella, Charlie."

"I'm afraid I agree with you, Preacher. Remember that funny track we saw when we went past where you had the tussle with Kenny that first day?" the sheriff asked.

"Yeah, one of his horse's hooves had a bent piece on the back, looked like the shoe was hit too hard with the mallet and bent it a bit. Not enough to hurt the horse's hoof, but it leaves an odd mark on the ground."

"Well, I found that same odd mark here. I'd have thought Kenny was smarter than that. You'd think he'd have seen it before now and realized that it was a signature of sorts. There's no doubt who we're looking for, far as I'm concerned. I'm thinking he's got him a place somewhere in the woods to hide out."

"Not a doubt in my mind," Simon said. "Come on up to the house when you've finished looking around, Sheriff. I'm going to let Grace know we'll be ready to eat in a short bit." Knowing she was doing her best to be patient, he headed back to the kitchen and the woman who was keeping a weather eye out on the backyard.

Her hands full, she watched him as he neared. A sack of cornmeal in one hand, a crock cradled against her waist containing eggs and a good measure of flour in the other, gave notice of her plans for supper. "You making corn bread, sweetheart?" he asked hopefully.

She cut a look his way that held a measure of

patience. "I suspect that's what all this looks like, Mr. Grafton. About twenty minutes ought to do it."

"We eating leftovers with it?" he asked

"Looks that way to me. Soup and corn bread, with pie for dessert."

"No complaints from me. And I'll guarantee Charlie will be happy as a clam. His housekeeper is neat and tidy, according to the sheriff, but can't cook worth a good gol durn."

He draped a long arm across her shoulders. "And I'll warrant there's not a man in town with a woman as pretty as you in his kitchen. But handy with a cookstove or not, so long as you meet me at the altar next week, I'll be a happy man."

Chapter Seven

It was past time to settle herself in bed, but Grace had headed for the parlor, unable to seek out the quiet comfort of her room. Ethel was long gone up the stairs and Simon had been bent over the library table, reading and scribbling ideas as fast as they entered his head.

"Are you about done for tonight?" she asked him quietly, aware that she disturbed his concentration, but unwilling to say her good-nights to him just yet.

"This can wait, Grace," he said, twisting his neck to relieve the tension of the past hour. "I've got it pretty well in hand, anyway. Come on in and join me, will you?"

"I just wanted to talk to you a bit, Simon." She stood behind him for a moment, her hands massaging the stiff muscles of his neck and shoulders.

"Thanks, sweetheart," he murmured as she ceased the movements of her hands and turned to sit on the sofa. In moments, he'd risen from his chair to join her.

"What are you fretting over, sweetheart?" he asked, twining an arm around her waist and drawing her back against himself.

"Not really fretting. Just wondering about the wedding." She was silent a moment and then shook her head. "No, it's more than that. I've been wondering what your expectations of me are, Simon. What do you need in a wife?"

It seemed her thoughts were much like his own, he decided. And he knew that matters needed to be spoken of before the wedding drew any closer. "I need to ask you something quite personal and private, Grace. I don't want to make you uncomfortable, but I need to know something. Did your mother speak with you about marriage—about sharing your life with a man?"

Grace shook her head slowly, looking rather dubious of his way of thinking. "We spoke of cooking and sewing. That sort of thing. Mama taught me how to put up vegetables from the garden, how to make my own clothing and drummed into me the general rules of good behavior.

"But when it came to marriage as it affects two

people, she seemed to feel embarrassed to speak of it. I remember asking her questions, but she was most reluctant to give me any answers. And then I came to live with Uncle Joe after Mama and Daddy died and there was no one there to talk to about such things."

"I feared as much," Simon said quietly. He held her hands in his and bent his head for a moment.

"Simon, are you praying?" she asked, stunned by the thought.

He grinned. "I probably should be, for I fear I have much to teach you, Grace, and I think I'm going to need divine help before I get through the maze I seem to be groping through."

"You've never been married, either, Simon. How did you ever find any answers?"

His voice was low, barely discernible as he spoke his thoughts. "There are some things that a man finds out in different ways than a woman does, Grace. I've probably had a few experiences in my life that you haven't been exposed to. I've gone out with young ladies for a number of years, both before I began college and then when I spent two years in seminary—and during that time I wasn't always an upright young fellow. Probably some would think that I made mistakes in my personal life, but I don't think I made any more than most young men. Given my years away from home and the influence of my family, I probably behaved pretty well. But I won't try to pull the wool over your eyes, dear one."

His pause was so long, Grace squeezed his hand and urged him to go on. "I'm not sure what you mean, Simon, but I think you'd better tell me just what it was you did in those years. I'm sure your education gained outside the walls of the schools you attended was more of a carnal nature than the teachings you learned from your educators."

"You've just about nailed the whole thing, Grace. There are temptations out in the world as we know it, that young men, especially, are prone to fall into. I was no different than many of my age, for I tried some of the pleasures offered to young folks everywhere."

"You went to saloons?" she asked, as if fearful of where this conversation was headed.

"A time or two. The taste of alcohol is not unknown to me, although I'm not a user of it nowadays. I remember smoking a cigar on two different occasions and got sicker than a skunk both times. So smoking was never a temptation after that."

"Did you try your hand at gambling?" she asked, her eyes wide as she attempted to peer into his, perhaps thinking she might see some sign of debauchery that lingered, even though he knew she had thought him to be honest and upright in his dealings.

Simon laughed softly. "I fear I tried the poker

tables and lost my proverbial shirt at the game. It hasn't tempted me since."

She shook her head. "I can't think of anything else you could have explored that might be considered beyond the pale for a young minister, Simon. Surely you didn't visit saloon girls, did you?"

He hesitated, his hands holding hers in a firm grip. "No, the women in the saloons never held any appeal, Grace, but there were a few young women who were available for the attentions of the young students where I went to school. I fear I took advantage of their charms, more than once. And then found that I was not satisfied with the idea of using a woman in such a way, that the truths in the Bible teach otherwise. And so I resolved to keep myself from temptation until I found a girl who might be a helpmate to me, who would want to share my life in the ministry. I wanted a woman I could love, a woman of depth and beauty, someone with high standards and the ability to work with me in my chosen profession."

"And do you think you've found such a woman in me?" she asked, feeling a bit inadequate to fill his needs.

"You're all I've ever wanted, Grace. You're not only lovely in your physical appearance, but your beauty goes deeper than that. You have a goodness of character I did not think to find in a girl of your young age. I've watched you within the walls of my home, seen how you work with Ethel and above and beyond that, I've not been able to ignore your beauty and the womanly ways you possess. Then, too, I've had a small taste of your loving spirit where I'm concerned. I won't ask for anything more from you for now, Grace. I want to keep you as innocent as you are right now, until our wedding night."

He bent to her then, his mouth seeking hers, his hands firm against her waist as he rose, holding her before him. He led her from the parlor then, carrying the lamp with him as they moved up the stairs and came to a halt outside Grace's bedroom door.

"I want badly to touch you again, Grace. To hold you close, to feel your body form to mine. I can't lie to you. It's difficult for me to want you so badly and not take some small bit for myself."

Grace lifted her face and kissed him, her mouth open against his lips, his cheeks. Then she whispered into the warmth of his throat. "You'll have the right whenever you want it, Simon, for I'm yours already. I'm anxious for the day to come when I'll become Mrs. Simon Grafton."

He chuckled softly and nipped at her ear. "I'll bet you wouldn't say those words to me in broad daylight, my little innocent. In fact, I'll warrant that your face is flaming even now."

"I know it is. I know I'm being forward, Simon.

I truly didn't think I could speak in such a fashion to a man."

"Ah, but I'm not just any man, love. I'm the man you're going to marry."

"I've never…" She looked up at him and then ducked her head. "I can't admit to any such experiences as you've had, Simon."

"I wouldn't have asked you for that information, Grace. That you offered it to me is a gift I appreciate more than you know. But there are things you need to know, sweetheart."

"Can't you tell me whatever that is?" she asked, as if unable to understand what there was that he didn't want to discuss with her.

His embrace was sudden, drawing her closer against himself, and Grace pressed her lips together lest she cry out and cause Ethel to awaken. With his mouth next to her ear, Simon whispered soft words that eased her mind.

"I'll tell you, but not now, not tonight. On our wedding night. We'll learn everything together, my love. For nothing I've ever experienced will come close to the joy I expect to find with you."

Her sigh was deep and she felt a thrill pass through her body unlike any she'd ever experienced in her life. "Simon, you make me feel happy, so… *wanted,* I suppose is the word."

"I do want you, sweetheart, more than you have any way of knowing. And one day, I hope you'll be able to tell me that you feel more than a liking for me, that your emotions will run to the depths of the promises we'll make to each other."

"The ones in the marriage service?" she asked

"All of those. The ones relating to honoring and cherishing your husband, for I can't ask you to obey me. I know that is the form of service most ministers use, but I'd rather know that you cherish what we share, than to have you sworn to obey me."

She clasped his neck, her face pressed into the front of his shirt. "I hope I don't disappoint you. I fear I'll find it difficult to…" She paused as if the words could not be spoken that would tell him of her fears. And then she whispered words that made him smile. "I can hear your heart beating, Simon. It's not very regular, is it?" she asked, her tone teasing.

"Not right now, sweetheart. But know that it's beating for you, for the knowledge that you'll be mine very soon, and we'll be together always."

Grace cracked the last of the eggs into a bowl and used a fork to whip them into shape. "I hope that Otto Crowder's got some fresh eggs in the general store today. We're out, and you can't keep a kitchen going without eggs," she told Simon.

"I'll go with you after a while," Simon said. "Or

else just make a list of what you need, and I'll stop by the Emporium and save you going out."

The eggs were scrambled, the bread toasted in the oven and the coffee was bubbling on the back burner when Simon went up the stairs to get Ethel. She was awaiting his arrival, dressed for the day in a clean starched housedress, all buttoned up, her slippers on and her face shiny from the warm water in her basin. To Simon's eyes, she seemed fully recovered from her close call.

"I believe I'm hungry," she said, taking Simon's arm and making her way down the stairway. They settled at the kitchen table and breakfast was served. Grace rose to clear up the dishes and Simon drank the last of his coffee.

He took his watch from its pocket and checked the time, then rose from the table. "I won't be gone for long, Grace, but I feel I need to go over to the saloon and see Belle. I'm thinking she could use some comfort right about now, and a bit of praying never hurt anyone."

"I've made a list, Simon," Grace said, pulling a piece of paper from the depths of her apron pocket. He took it, noting the items and nodding as he put it in his pocket.

"I'll stop on my way to see Belle, and then when I'm done there, your things should be all packed up in a box for me to bring home." He bent and kissed her quickly and left by the back door, Grace locking it behind him.

"Well, I'd better start thinking about getting ready for a wedding," Ethel said, watching as Grace poured hot water into the pan in the sink where the breakfast dishes waited. "You'll be busy at the church a good share of the time after the wedding, Grace. I think you'll have your hands full with the ladies' missionary group and all. Bet they'll have you teaching a Sunday school class, too," Ethel said. "I'll send word to a couple of the ladies and let them know that I'll be needing a bit of help for a few days, making plans for your reception and all."

Grace flushed brightly at Ethel's words. "I didn't think of all that. I'm taking on more than just a husband, aren't I? Our pastor's wife back home when I was a girl used to organize all the church socials and the wedding showers when one of the young ladies was married. She had to keep flowers in the church, too. Every Sunday morning there were fresh bouquets on the communion table. Being a minister's wife means more than taking on a new name."

Ethel laughed. "Don't get all stirred up yet, missy. Those ladies will have them a time, lending a hand and offering help with things. I know Maude Parker is a right hand with quilting. You just ask her and I'd be willing to guarantee she'll take over the quilting bees. It'll make her feel important, and take a load off you. And when it comes time to putting together a church social, you just ask Mabel Hicks how she makes her marble cake and she'll volunteer to be in charge of all the cake-baking, you watch and see. And Lettie Proctor is the best woman in town when it comes to providing volunteers for making up baskets at Christmastime for those who need help."

"Oh, Ethel! What on earth would I do without you? You'll have to help me to bring all those names to mind. I'm going to need you, that's for certain. I'll never remember all that you just told me."

"Well, we'll just put our heads together whenever the need arises, Grace. It's not any problem at all and I'll be here to help you in any way I can."

"My life will be so different." Grace took a deep breath, her hands rising to cover her cheeks. "My world's all changed around, Ethel. I wonder what my mama would say if she knew what all has happened to me."

"I reckon she'd be tickled to death, girl. Ain't every day a young woman gets courted by a preacher, and finds a new place in life. Both her and your daddy are no doubt happy for you."

"Do you suppose they know?"

Ethel nodded. "I'm no great authority, but there's more goes on in the afterlife than any of us earthlings got any clue of. How do we know whether or not our happiness don't kinda leak over onto the other side? I'd like to think your mama knows you're happy, Gracie. She sure couldn't have asked any better for you than to meet Simon and for him to fall head over heels for you. He looks at you like you're the best thing since…well, since clothespins was invented."

Grace hung the dish towel she'd used over the front of the sink and turned to face Ethel. "My head is all awhirl with things, Ethel. What with the wedding coming up so quickly, I'm in a dither."

"Don't you worry about all that," the housekeeper said soothingly. "Everything will fall into place."

"Well, I know he's set the date. It's to be Saturday next," Grace said softly. "He's already let his folks know and the bishop has agreed to come. Did you hear Simon when he spoke of letting the deacons at the church know of his plans? He felt a marriage would solve the problem of gossip being widespread, for he's more than aware of the danger of folks not recognizing the need of my staying here with you both."

"Well, I think it'll all work out just fine, Grace. And now it's our job to get busy planning a nice wedding for the two of you. The ladies in town will be pleased to arrange the details of the reception. All we need to do is let them know what your plans are and they'll take over. Simon is a good man and his congregation will be happy for him."

So easily it was done, Grace thought, sitting on the edge of her bed an hour later looking around the room she would be moving from, in order to sleep in Simon's bedroom from now on. The handmade quilt she sat on no doubt came from the hands of the women Simon served and the oval rug by the bed displayed the talents of one of the women from the church. She was surrounded with evidence of Simon's standing in the community, for even the crocheted doilies on the dresser had been gifts from some lady in his congregation.

She opened the long drawer in her dresser and then looked up into the mirror provided for her use. She was flushed, her hair needed attention and confusion had set her thoughts scrambling. First things first, she decided, reaching for her brush, bringing a semblance of order to the strands that had escaped her hastily constructed braid. After a moment's brushing and another few minutes spent with a cloth and warm water, she felt better able to go back downstairs.

Hearing sounds in the kitchen, she went through the doorway, to find Ethel sitting at the kitchen table, that lady intent on making plans, already armed with a pencil and a piece of paper. As if organizing a wedding must be of utmost importance, Ethel seemed eager to plunge into arrangements, and Ethel Anderson on a mission was something to behold, Grace decided almost immediately.

In fact, within half an hour Ethel had managed to plan all but the bridal bouquet. But as she said, she'd make it herself and the bouquet would be a surprise for Grace.

"If Simon can fit us into his day, we'll go to the Emporium tomorrow and find a dress for you or else some pretty fabric I can sew up. We have time to make a lovely dress, Grace, so if there isn't one ready-made that will suit us, we can just make our own." Ethel summed up her plans and waited for Grace's approval.

"That sounds fine to me. I'm rather new at this sort of thing, so I'll bow to your superior judgment, Ethel," Grace said with a soft sound of laughter.

It was almost an hour later when Simon entered the front door of the parsonage, his voice calling out to the two women in his household. The sound of her name on his lips was more than welcome to Grace. She'd been dusting the wooden pieces in the parlor, wiping picture frames and fluffing the pillows on the sofa. There was little left for her to do in the house, for Ethel was determined she should not labor overmuch at housework.

And now Simon stood in the doorway, his gaze seeking her out, a box of supplies from the general store in his arms and his demeanor that of a man shaken to his core. It was obvious to Grace that he was upset beyond belief at the sight he had just been privy to in the room over the saloon. His face was white and strained, and furrows lined his brow.

"It could have been you, Grace. He could have damaged you the way he hurt Belle, and even though I ache for her pain, I can only be thankful that you were spared such an amount of abuse," he said quietly, carrying the groceries to the kitchen and then turning to Grace. His arms went around her. Held so closely in his embrace, she was able to feel the trembling he could not contain.

"It was all I could think of when I left her, that you might have been the one with broken ribs. I've tried not to ever hate another human being, but I'm not sure I can face this test. If God truly wants me to be his servant, I'll need help in dealing with my anger."

"I'm so sorry, Simon. Not just for Belle, but for you, too. My injuries healed quickly and I'm thankful. You see so much of the bad in life, and yet on Sunday morning, you must face your congregation and offer them hope for their future and the promise of love from the Heavenly Father. And all the time, you must be wondering how He can allow such things to happen."

Two tears slid down her cheeks as Grace tried to express her thoughts to Simon, and he could only hold her closely, his need for her apparent. He drew her into the parlor, then sat with her on the sofa, his arms still surrounding her, his lips touching her face, the faint rasp of his whiskers against her cheeks making her smile as he held her near. He leaned back after a few moments and his gaze touched hers.

"I seem to spend a lot of time with my arms around you of late, Grace. I hope you don't mind."

She shook her head. "You know I don't, Simon. I enjoy your kisses and the feel of you close to me."

"Grace, I know you have some bad memories of things that have happened in your past. I'm trying to keep that in mind as we approach our wedding. I don't want you to be fearful of me or what we will share after we're married," he said. "And you've certainly known harsh treatment at the hands of at least one man. I'm trying to take all of that into account when I think of the beginning of our marriage."

"I'll do my best to be what you want, Simon. But I'm not certain I feel equipped to be the wife of a minister. There's a lot more to it than even you seem to understand," she said. "But I'll do my best to support you and do my part. I hope you know that."

"I do, Grace, and I appreciate it more than you'll ever know." His smile was warm, the mood lighter as he began to speak of his part in getting ready for their wedding.

"I'm going to get a crew of men together the day before the wedding. We'll spend a couple of hours getting the church ready for the big day. And I'll need to get a new tie. Seems like I ought to have a new shirt, too."

"I can take care of both items easily, Preacher. Don't forget Ethel and I are going to the Emporium tomorrow."

"Do you feel like taking a walk with me right now?" he asked, and she beamed a smile in his direction.

They left the parsonage then, walking down the road to the train station where Simon inquired as to an answer to his wire. The stationmaster shook his head and laughed.

"Hardly enough time for them to send one, Preacher. Try again tomorrow."

Simon grinned sheepishly and nodded. "I'm an anxious groom it seems. I'll be back tomorrow."

Grace looked up at him as they strolled back to the parsonage, aware that his attention was on their surroundings, his gaze on the lookout for problems should they arise.

"I don't mean to hurry you along," he said with a chuckle, his hand holding hers as they made their way back to the parsonage. But Simon lengthened his stride as he encouraged Grace to move more quickly. He felt exposed, as if eyes watched them, and his spine was chilled, realizing how fragile life was with danger all about. Simon yearned for the safety he'd taken for granted for so long.

He held open the gate for her to step into the front yard and together they went up the walk to the porch, Grace coming to a dead halt and uttering a sound that was almost a scream, stepping back, almost falling from the single step.

For there, lying on the stoop, atop the mat placed to wipe boots or shoes upon, was a bouquet of weeds tied with string. A mockery of her wedding bouquet was all that Grace could think of. Simon reached down and snatched up a piece of paper from the midst of the dried weeds, and opened it, reading the scrawled lines and then crumpling it within his palm. He gathered the obscene bundle of weeds in one hand and turned Grace from the porch.

"Oh, Simon, who would do such a thing?" she cried aloud, tears rolling down her cheeks as she thought of the mockery of what would be so large a part of her wedding day. "What did the note say?"

"Never mind, Grace. We're taking it to the sheriff right now and giving it to him."

"Was it intended for me?" she asked, knowing even before she spoke the words that there was no doubt as to who the intended recipient was.

"I'm afraid so." Supporting her with one long arm around her waist, he led her from the porch.

They crossed the road and in moments were at the jailhouse. Simon opened the door, startling Charlie Wilson, who rose from his chair hurriedly. "What's wrong, Simon?"

"This was left on my porch." Simon gave him the crumpled bit of paper and placed the weeds on his desk. He watched as the sheriff straightened the note to read it.

"What the hell is this?" he growled, and then looked at Grace with a sheepish grin. "Sorry, ma'am. Didn't mean to cuss that way, but you must have been about shocked out of your shoes to see this."

"Simon wouldn't show me the note. Looking at the weeds was bad enough. They were left for us to find. We'd just returned from the train station."

Charlie muttered darkly beneath his breath for a moment, then turned to the man who watched him, awaiting his opinion. "Well, it was no doubt intended for her eyes, Simon, and she'd might as well know what sort of a—"

As if he thought better of the term he was about to use, Charlie turned to Grace. "It says he hopes you'll think of him while you enjoy his bouquet of flowers. Stupid bas—" Charlie swallowed the word, unspoken.

He crumpled the note, then as if thinking better

of it, unfolded it and smoothed it against the surface of his desk before slipping it into the center drawer.

"We'll just save that to show the judge when he gets here. I'll put this mess in the back room," he said, lifting the weeds and carrying them through the doorway to his storage area. "Just wish I had a prisoner for him to haul back with him."

"Nothing yet?" Simon asked, almost without hope, for this was a daily query.

Charlie shook his head. "No sign of him yet. Joe offered to have his men watching for him, even the fellas up at the line shack, north of here. He seems to have had a change of heart about things. It's about time, I'd say."

"Well, at least he's willing to cooperate to that extent. I thought for a while he wouldn't even do that," Simon said, his tone angry, his eyes sharp as he spoke of Grace's uncle. "Grace sent him a note, inviting him to the wedding. She doesn't want any hard feelings with Joe to darken our wedding day. And Joe seemed pleased to get a special invitation."

"I think he's decided to do the best he can to find the fella, Simon. But Kenny knows we're after him, and he's a slippery one, that's for sure. But unless he's left the area, we'll find him or he'll give himself away, one way or another."

"Well, Miss Grace and I have a wedding to plan,

sir, and I'd like to ask you to stand up with me in church. Kinda give me your moral support."

Charlie looked more than pleased. "That would be an honor, Simon. I'll wear my best bib and tucker for the event."

Grace was silent as they walked back to the parsonage, and Simon's anger was stirred against the fates that seemed to destroy her happiness.

"It will work out, Grace. We'll make our plans and have a lovely wedding, no matter what. Ethel is excited about the reception and her mood will be contagious when she speaks to the ladies at church on Sunday. I've seen a wedding here before and those women are real slick when it comes to putting on a meal and feeding the whole town. Which will be the case next week. I guarantee it, sweetheart."

Chapter Eight

The church was hushed, each pew packed almost to its limit, and the groom waited before the altar, the local lawman beside him. His bishop had come gladly to the village church in Maple Creek, Kansas, presenting a solemn figure as he stood with a slender black volume in his hands watching Grace walk down the aisle. Ethel had preceded her and stood now just to the left of where Simon awaited his bride.

He watched as she neared, this lovely girl who had promised to be his wife. In the front pew on either side of the aisle sat two older couples, his parents on the right, Harold and Ellie Blackwood on the left. Ellie's arm was healed, her sling left behind, and she was pleased as punch, so she'd said upon arrival at the church. Being invited to the wedding of their young minister obviously pleased her, for Simon had dropped by the farm days ago and brought a handwritten note from Grace, one of several Simon delivered.

What looked like the whole town arrayed in their finest was seated in the remaining spaces. A latecomer to the ceremony, limping a bit, was a buxom blonde lady who was recognized by several men of the congregation as Miss Belle. Being from the saloon, she was looked at askance by several and ignored by many. But it seemed she wanted to be present at the wedding of the man who had been so kind to her during her convalescence, for she'd made it known that his visit to her had encouraged her, no matter that he had entered the saloon to make his call. Though Belle still bore damaged skin from the beating she'd received, a heavy veil over her face concealed much, and her broken arm was in a sling, held close against her chest.

The bride was lovely, her white dress falling from a narrow waist, caught up at the hem with satin roses, made expressly for the occasion by Ethel and sewn in place just hours ago. Grace was a fitting name for this slender, feminine creature who smiled at Simon, as even now the organ played a triumphant hymn. Joy dwelled on her lips, illuminating her face as though a ray of sunshine had come to be captured there in the glowing cheeks.

Light shimmered through the dark waves and curls that fell over her shoulders and down her back.

She carried flowers from his garden, a blend of roses and lilies, of greenery and tiny white blossoms. A pink ribbon wove between the stems and was tied into a generous bow, the work of his housekeeper, for Simon had seen her at dawn, picking the blossoms and preparing the bouquet Grace would carry. Now he was pleased that she seemed to have put from her mind the ugly token left on the doorstep only days past.

Grace looked up then, directly into his eyes and her smile, though it trembled on her lips, was a thing of beauty, a precious gift that spoke of her commitment to him, a prequel to the vows they would speak.

And it was the earnest cry of Simon's heart that he might provide Grace with years of joy, for he felt a great need of her, a heartfelt yearning that he might be the source of her happiness in the years to come.

She was to be his wife. *His*. And Simon felt his chest expand with pride as she met him before the altar. They had decided that she would walk alone down the aisle, that she would offer herself to him as a woman. For should she have asked him, Harold Blackwood would have gladly given her in marriage; even her uncle would have been pleased to give her away, for he'd said as much to Simon when the preacher had gone to the ranch to issue the invitation to the wedding.

Uncle Joe had finally recognized that his original choice of a husband for Grace was not a viable option, for, to all accounts, Kenny had proved himself to be a ruffian; that fact Joe accepted. Grace was far better off as the wife of a man with prospects, for Simon was indeed a man much admired in the community. And Joe had told him just that, the day he offered to walk Grace down the aisle to meet her groom. It seemed that Joe and his niece were heading for a better relationship.

But Grace was determined on this one small thing. She would give *herself* to Simon.

That she was doubting her ability to be a minister's wife, a helpmate to Simon, was uppermost in her mind. But she had come thus far and was more than ready to be just what Simon needed and wanted in a wife. The giving of herself into his keeping was important to her—a vow of her love.

The words they spoke now were ancient, the cadence familiar to those listening, but the vows were fresh and new to Simon. Though he had spoken them before while conducting such a service for others, today they took on new meaning. For today, they were *his* vows, *his* promises, and Grace was forever and always to be his wife.

Though the kiss was expected, the congregation

sighed as one as Simon's lips touched hers. As his eyes cut down and met hers, a single word of promise was spoken for only his bride to hear.

"Later."

And she knew, for her blush told him she understood that vow as well as those preceding it. Later he would make her his own. Later they would lie in the big bed in his room and seek out the mysteries of marriage. And at that thought, Grace trembled.

But for now, Simon turned her to face his congregation and together they walked from the sanctuary, where the silence was finally broken by the whispering of a hundred lips, the shuffling of as many feet and the impatience of children who were anxious for the party to begin.

For their parents had no doubt told them of the feast awaiting them at the parsonage. Of chicken and dumplings, vegetables and roast beef, the bread, baked just that morning in homes all over town, and then the final touch.

The wedding cake was four tiers in all, with pink roses and green leaves arrayed on each layer, the bottom tier resplendent on a large board from the lumberyard. A board Ethel had covered with lace doilies before setting her masterpiece in place.

Simon had caught a glimpse of it just an hour past, as he looked into his dining room at the table awaiting the platters and bowls of food the ladies of the town would furnish for his bridal feast. He felt humbled by their kindness, the generosity of his people, and now, as he walked into the sunshine, he was caught up in the beauty of the girl he had married.

She looked at him and smiled, and he bent to her, his mouth briefly touching hers, not wanting to share his thoughts with any but her for this moment. "Hello, Mrs. Grafton," he murmured, and then liking the sound of that only too well, he continued. "You're Grace Grafton. From now on, you'll bear my name, sweetheart."

And it was right and proper that she touch his cheek and, in front of all the townspeople who streamed from the double doors of his church, she drew his face down to kiss him, a mere touch of her lips to his, but a promise he cherished with his whole heart.

The reception was noisy, the company of his parents and even Grace's uncle Joe welcome. Simon's heart rejoiced when he saw Joe approach Grace, take her hands and bend to touch his lips to her cheek. The words he spoke were soft, but Simon was pleased to see Grace smile and welcome her uncle's approach. And Joe's words to her were gracious, an offering of peace that would heal the wounds between them.

"I'm sorry, Grace. I was wrong about you and Kenny. Please forgive me."

Grace nodded and smiled joyfully as she hugged her uncle, whispering words that made the man nod and then lift his head high, as if he had set aside a great burden. And so he had, Simon thought, feeling at peace.

Simon's mother, Cora, dried her eyes, looking up at Simon with pride and then speaking to Grace of her gown and bouquet. His father, George, clasped his hand and offered congratulations, whispering in his ear that he'd made his mother happy today, for she could foresee a whole flock of grandchildren in her future.

Simon shared a plate of food with Grace, although neither of them did credit to the tempting morsels he'd chosen to tempt her palate. They sat on the porch swing, his toe moving the green, freshly painted vehicle back and forth, receiving the well wishes of their friends.

And all the time, he resisted the urge to check his watch, only twice pulling it from his pocket to note the slow movement of the hands that measured his wedding day. For if ever a man was impatient with the tolling clock in the dining room, if ever a groom was eager for his guests to leave, it was Simon. He minded his manners, obeying Grace's almost silent warning as she whispered to him.

"You'll only have one wedding day, Simon. Enjoy it. Look at your mother…how pleased she is. And how proud your father is of you."

He bent to her again, his lips touching her ear as he whispered back, words he was glad no one else could hear. "All I want to enjoy right now, Grace… is you."

She blushed furiously at that and he laughed, a soft chuckle that caused her to bow her head lest those who watched them would know of what he spoke. And as Simon looked around, he was aware that the menfolk, at least, knew very well his impatience, and perhaps understood.

And then the time came when the last guest left, his parents returned to the hotel where he'd reserved them a room, the townsfolk to their homes and Harold and Ellie, the last to leave, finally were driven home in their buggy by their hired hand, Scooter, who preened at his important role today.

The house was quiet, Ethel having left after the reception to visit her daughter for a day or so. And in the twilight, Simon led Grace to his bedroom, where clean sheets and crisp new pillowcases awaited her comfort. One of his parishioners had embroidered bright yellow-and-purple pansies on the hems and then starched and ironed them to pristine beauty.

Grace exclaimed over them, her fingers touching the fine stitches, her eyes alight with pleasure at the gift. Simon had another gift for her, one he'd bought at the general store just yesterday, when for a few moments the store was thankfully empty of all customers but himself.

Mr. Crowder had smiled broadly as he showed Simon his assortment of sleepwear for women and approved his minister's choice when he'd pointed to a muslin specimen, adorned with lace, a gown looking likely to fit his bride-to-be. And now he went to his dresser and opened his drawer, lifting the pale gown in his hands and offering it to Grace.

"Will you wear this for me?" he asked, and watched as she held it up and whispered soft words of thanks. That she held it in the moonlight from the window was pure chance, he decided, for he knew she hadn't planned it that way, but the knowledge that the sheer fabric would not hide her charms from him was almost more than his masculine needs could withstand.

She took it behind the folding screen in one corner of his room, where his washbasin and pitcher sat, freshly scrubbed and filled with hot water by Ethel before she took her leave. He heard Grace splashing the water into the basin, knew when she used the washcloth provided for her and watched as her dress was tossed over the top of the screen.

As she stepped into his sight after but a few moments, the moonlight outside their bedroom window made Grace appear as a slender wraith before him.

He'd stripped from his shirt and tie, left the jacket of his suit across the clothes tree in the hallway, and now he watched as Grace stood silently waiting. It was almost more than he could bear, the innocent beauty of her, dark hair falling to her waist, her eyes curious, yet wary. For she was truly an innocent.

Though she'd known that she was attractive to him, and to others, in this Grace was facing the unknown. She'd told him of boys and men who had sought her out as a young girl, who'd praised her beauty and perhaps yearned to own it.

She'd felt the cruel hands of a man on her flesh, yet she looked at Simon now with trust, for though she might not understand what was to come, she had faith that Simon would make all things beautiful for her tonight. Yet, a nagging fear crept in, setting loose a trembling she could not control. Simon had promised her many things, his care of her, his patience, his arms to hold and protect her. And Grace was determined to be all that he needed, all that he wanted tonight. She could not fail him in this.

Her face was a pale oval, for the room was unlit but for the rising moon and the few stars that shone in awakening splendor across the darkening sky. And yet there was a faint smile there, a gentle curve of her lips that told him she was his, even though she trembled in his arms. He lifted her against himself, feeling the soft curves of her breasts against his chest, the length of her legs against his, as he picked her up, cradling her in his arms, and turned to the bed.

Gently, he placed her against the pillows, the quilt already tossed to the foot of the bed. She reached for the sheet, but he would not have it and hushed her small sounds of protest as he took it from her and let it fall over the quilt. And then he slid his trousers and drawers down his legs and shed them on the floor. With a whispered word that spoke of her beauty, he lay down beside her, his body touching hers with a familiarity she had never known. And he felt her indrawn breath, her soft murmur of denial as she shrank back from him.

"Grace? Don't be frightened of me. I won't hurt you, sweetheart," he whispered.

But he was without clothing, and the only barrier between the softness of her breasts and hips and his own flaring need was the sheer fabric of a gown that offered little protection to the girl who wore it. He would not frighten her by taking it from her, for this night would be long and he had plans that did not include fear on Grace's part or any haste on his own. And yet he sensed that she withdrew from him, her body moving so that it no longer touched his.

Simon frowned, aching to reassure her, yet unable to understand her reticence. He lifted himself up over her, bending to look into her eyes, speaking words he'd never before found in his vocabulary, for as a younger man, Simon had sought out women for needs that precluded words such as *love*. And now that word loomed large in his mind, for he recognized that tonight there was much more than a simple need for fulfillment, more than a yearning for her feminine flesh in this coming together.

He ached to know her as his wife, yet enough caution still abode in his rapidly escaping sensibility to woo her gently. And so his hands were careful, his touch tender as he learned the lines of her body, his fingers slow and careful as he lifted her gown.

"Simon, don't take my gown from me," she whispered, her voice almost hoarse in the stillness.

He moved over her, careful not to make her feel helpless beneath him. "I only want to touch you, Grace, to feel your softness. But I'll leave your gown on if you feel the need." Her legs were slender and he ran his hand down the length of her calf, grasping her slender foot and looking down at the toes that curled against his palm.

She was trembling in his arms and he would not have it, for he wanted no fear to damage this night for her. And yet there was his need to touch, to see.

Her gown opened easily, the small buttons sliding from their moorings, her bodice spread open, exposing the pale upper slopes of her breasts. He bent then, his mouth touching the skin there, the soft curving beauty of her. She inhaled sharply as his mouth moved a bit, his lips opening over the tender crest that responded to his tongue.

She shivered and gasped. "Simon…no, please. Don't do that."

She wasn't ready for this, he realized, and lifted his head, his hand smoothing the placket of her gown in place. And then, wonder of wonders, he felt her hands lift to touch the back of his head, knew the pressure of slender fingers against his dark hair, ruffling through that hair until she clasped him close to her, bringing his face to hers.

"Simon, I'm sorry. I want to be your wife, but I didn't expect you to—"

"It's all right, Grace. I understand. I moved too quickly and didn't take your modesty into consideration."

"Forgive me, Simon. I don't mean to push you away. I just need a few minutes to realize what you expect of me."

"Only that you allow me the privilege of being your husband, of making you my wife, Grace.

I won't do anything to frighten you if I can help it."

Her eyes were wide in the shadows of twilight, her lips trembling, and she spoke his name softly. "Simon."

It was only the speaking of his name, but the voice was that of his beloved, and he inhaled the scent of her, knew the taste of her and blessed her with the caresses he'd longed to bestow upon her, limited though they were.

That he touched only her face was a disappointment to him, but he swallowed it readily, lest she turn from him. So his kiss was not as ardent as he wished, but rather that of a supplicant, soft and seeking the warmth of her mouth. She turned her face to his, meeting his lips with her own, and her moan of delight was almost silent. But he knew it for what it was, and rejoiced at the pleasure she was not fearful of expressing to him.

"You're so soft, yet firm, Grace. I've wanted so long to touch you here…" His hand enclosed her breast, his palm cupping her through the fabric of her gown. "And here…" His fingers slid to the hem of her gown, lifting it a bit to touch her thigh, his fingers brushing the length of it.

"Don't be frightened, Grace. I only want to touch you," he whispered against her throat, and felt the rapid beat of her heart in the soft flesh there. His hand slipped upward, skimming her hip and then lying flat against her stomach. He felt the soft tuft of curls that protected her feminine parts on the edge of his palm and somehow knew that she would not allow him to trespass further.

"Please, Grace." He waited for her acquiescence, for though he could have parted her legs easily with a movement of his hand, he waited for her to offer herself to him.

But it was not to be, for she whispered her denial aloud. "Simon. I don't think I can do what you want. Not tonight. I just can't."

He felt her trembling, knew she was more than fearful of what he might do, and with a determination he had not known he possessed, he pulled her gown back down over her legs and settled beside her.

"Just let me hold you, Grace. Put your head on my shoulder and lie beside me."

"All right," she whispered, shifting to do as he'd asked, lying beside him with his arms around her.

He felt her shiver and pulled the sheet up to cover her, his head bending, so that he might kiss her with soft caresses meant to ease her fright.

He was being denied a wedding night, and the pain of that denial struck him with sharp talons, rending his spirits until he felt himself falling into the depths of despair. He had frightened his bride, had failed in his wooing of her.

"Perhaps tomorrow night, Simon," she whispered softly. "I'll truly try to do better."

"I was at fault, Grace. I rushed you too much, and frightened you."

"I'm not afraid of *you,* Simon. Only of what you expect of me. I think I wasn't aware of how intimate this would be. I should have known."

"How could you?" he asked, only now realizing just how innocent his bride truly was. She'd had no one to speak with her about this act of marriage, and he'd thought he could persuade her to fill the part of a wife. And perhaps he could, but not tonight, he realized.

His hand moved to her back and he smoothed a wrinkle from her gown, his fingers against the fabric, his hand moving in a soothing pattern. She murmured soft words he did not understand, perhaps whispering a good-night to him, he thought, and then she snuggled a bit closer, as if she'd lost her fear of his touch. In mere moments, she was sleeping, not a sound slumber, but apparently she trusted him enough to lie beside him and curl closely to his long form.

Simon's eyes closed for a moment, and then snapped open again, for he was only too aware that this night would be long. He was married, and yet not a husband. And with little to look forward to, unless Grace could be persuaded to speak with Ethel. The girl needed to have a womanly conversation with someone, for it didn't appear Simon could persuade her to his will.

And so he lay, awake and silent, aware only of the slight weight of Grace by his side, his manhood aching and needy.

He must have fallen asleep, for when he next stirred, Grace was gone from his bed, the pillow still warm where her head had been, the sheet pushed aside and only the rays of the rising sun sharing the place where he lay.

After breakfast they walked into town. Simon did not have to preach the morning service at church; his bishop had offered to tend to it in his stead. His parents were sitting on the porch at the hotel, rocking in chairs provided there for the guests who shared the hospitality of the establishment. Simon's parents expressed a wish to treat Simon and his bride to a meal in the hotel dining room, and shortly after noon they found themselves sitting around a table, perusing the handwritten menu with Sunday's offerings listed.

After ordering, they settled down to await their meal and Simon's mother shared her delight in the amenities offered by the hotel. She laughed softly, speaking of the buckets of water carried up the long flight of stairs by the bellboy, then dumped into a private bathing tub, the treat arranged for her pleasure by Simon's father. And when that gentleman smiled at Cora Grafton, it was obvious to both Simon and Grace that George was bewitched by his wife of over thirty years.

They ate well. Simon especially was hungry, for his wedding feast had not been properly appreciated; only the time with his bride had been important yesterday. Now he demolished a steak, watched as Grace ate chicken potpie and shared small talk with his mother over their dinner. His mother spoke of home, of his childhood friends, of family members and of their train ride, finding Grace to be a good listener, for she was eager to hear anything his mother had to say about Simon.

Simon was aware that his mother had traveled but little in her life, only to the next county, there in Oklahoma, and the train traveling the distance to Maple Creek, Kansas, must have seemed like a magical time to her. She was but a simple woman, a loving mother and a wife of whom his father could be proud. And he found that such things mattered more to him today than they had before.

Perhaps it was having a wife of his own that opened his eyes to the beauty of womanhood, that made him more aware of his own mother's loveliness, faded a bit over the years, but still vibrant and pleasing.

They would stay for the evening vespers service in his church, for though the bishop had served in Simon's pulpit this morning, he was even now on his way back home and Simon would handle the vespers tonight.

And now they left the hotel dining room, Simon's parents vowing they would enjoy the quiet of a Sunday and perhaps steal a nap in their lovely room on the second floor. For Simon, there was the joy of walking through town with his bride on his arm, catching her clean, sweet scent as he bent to her and spoke of many things.

They sauntered slowly, aware of watching eyes, for some of the townsfolk were blatant in their survey of the young couple. Many sat on porches, enjoying the summer day, several buggies passed them by and hands were lifted in greeting. Simon felt pride steal over him, though he knew that it could be a besetting sin, this feeling of arrogance that filled him as he looked down at his wife. Surely no man had ever had such beauty by his side, such sweetness to bear up in his arms as he carried her over their threshold.

It might be a day late, but Simon had decided to observe the custom, lifting Grace into his arms and opening the front door to carry her into the foyer before he set her down on the floor. "I meant to do that yesterday, but I was so eager to get you home, I forgot," he said with a chuckle. He pushed the door closed behind them and took her in his arms, yearning for her hands on his face, her lips touching his, the sweet scent of woman filling him to overflowing.

They took a nap of their own then, although Grace said later that he hadn't slept much, only held her and whispered soft words to her as she dozed. They arose in time for vespers at the church, and Simon took his place behind his pulpit. He led his congregation in prayer, directed them in hymns from the hymnals and spoke but a few words of scripture, as befitted a vespers service. His final words were of thanksgiving for his church, his people and his parents, who had guided his life into the path he now took.

And then he dismissed his congregation and met them, one and all, at the wide front doors of his church, shaking hands, speaking small bits of greeting in the manner he'd grown to enjoy.

And by his side stood the woman of his choice, she of the laughing eyes and flashing dimples. Her dark hair was formed into a mass of curls and pinned atop her head, and if he thought of its beauty spread across his pillow, he could be forgiven, he supposed, for it was enough to tempt a saint, to think of her thusly.

And Simon Grafton was no saint.

Chapter Nine

Monday morning found them on the train platform, waving as George and Cora Grafton stood at
the back of the final railway car, the last of a long
line following the smoke-spewing engine. Simon's
mother wiped away a tear, and his father slid his
arm around her waist and tugged her close, win-
ning a smile from her for his efforts.

The train pulled away and Simon swallowed
hard as his parents disappeared. He'd made his
choice to settle in Maple Creek years ago, but
their leaving was wrenching since he saw them so
seldom. It was the knowledge that they had come
so far to see him married that tempered his sadness
at their departure.

Grace took his arm and turned him away from
the platform. He looked down into her face and

reveled once more in his own good fortune. She was comforting him when her own parents had been dead and buried for over a year, and she would never see them again. His smile was not feigned as he led her toward home, for he recognized again the blessings he'd so recently been gifted.

They were halted midway through town when the sheriff hailed them from in front of the jailhouse. "Did your parents get off all right?" he asked Simon and then ushered them into his office.

"I need to let you know that we're having a tough time finding Kenny Summers, folks. I went out to the Cumberland place again, and it seems he's not been seen there since just before Belle got mauled so bad over at the saloon. You need to know to be careful. The man is a fugitive now and unless he's left town altogether, he's more than likely a danger to Grace."

"I wouldn't count on him walking away," Simon said ruefully.

"Nor would I," Charlie Wilson agreed.

Grace felt her heart almost leap into her throat. "You don't think he'd hurt Harold or Ellie, or any of the elderly folks outside of town, do you, Sheriff? He might think to get back at me that way, since I was at the Blackwoods' farm, even though it was but for a few hours one day. He might have followed us there."

"It's hard telling how his mind works, Grace.

We've solid proof of him being responsible for the attack on Belle, for she's ready to identify him in court, so I think his days of freedom are numbered. Once we get ahold of him, he'll spend a good long time in jail."

Their walk as they continued through town was quiet, their mood sober as they thought of the pain and suffering of Belle. Grace's words burst from her as though they could not be contained. "I almost wish your bullet had been lower the day you shot Kenny. If it had struck him in the chest, we might not have all these problems, Simon."

He shook his head. "You don't know how I struggled with what happened that day. I had to preach a sermon on one of the commandments the following Sunday. I was doing a series and the next one in line was relating to murder."

Grace halted and clutched at Simon's arm. "But you didn't kill him, Simon. I should be ashamed, for I was wrong to even wish such a thing. And I well remember that sermon. And all the rest of the commandments that followed on the Sunday mornings after that."

"No, I didn't kill him, but I fear I wanted to," Simon admitted. He looked away from Grace, as if he could not face her with the admission. "And if I had, it would have been better all the way around. I have to admit, I agree with you, sweetheart. It would have been more fit and proper an ending had I aimed a bit lower that day. Poor Belle would not still be suffering from his attack."

"I don't recall you aiming that day, Simon. You just held your gun and shot it. I doubt you even thought about where the bullet would hit him."

He looked at her in silence for a moment and then, grasping her hand, continued on down the road toward the parsonage. "You can't imagine how difficult it was for me to have to tell my bishop what I'd done, Grace. He didn't hold me accountable, for he said any man would have done the same. But I've felt, ever since I chose my profession, that as a man pledged to serve God, I must set my standards higher than just any other fellow in the world. I remember when I was younger, how I felt about our pastor back home, how I admired him and his principles.

"I suppose that's one reason why I couldn't have taken your innocence before our wedding. It wouldn't have been right for me. I don't judge anyone else, only Simon Grafton, and for me there has to be a set of rules to follow."

"I fear even now you've been robbed of your rightful loving of me, Simon. I'm so sorry to be such a coward, for you're a good man and deserved better from me," Grace said quietly, her head bowed.

Simon thought then of his failings in life, knowing that Grace thought him to be an almost perfect man, and that was far from the truth. He spoke impetuously then, telling her of the man he'd killed so long ago as a youth, and in a few short words he made Grace aware of the incident. For he wanted his conscience clear, feeling that she deserved to know the worst of him.

And yet, the light of love still shone from her blue eyes. "God doesn't expect any of us to be perfect, Simon, but defending your mother that day was the act of a loving son," Grace said simply. She felt his pain, knowing that he'd fallen short of his own standards on that day so long ago. And again on the day he'd wounded Kenny. She smiled up at him, swinging their hands between them as they walked, hoping to lighten his mood a bit, speaking of their earlier discussion. "And did you enjoy finishing the series on the Ten Commandments, Simon?"

He grinned. "Yeah, the rest weren't nearly so difficult for me to preach. But I'll admit I'm finding it easier to work on the good guys in the Bible right now. I'm devoting a Sunday morning to each of them, starting with Noah a month or so ago. Although he was no saint, either, now that I think about it. I guess there aren't too many of them floating around these days, any more than there were back then."

"You may be right, but then I have to admit I'm rather prejudiced in your favor." Her smile was brilliant, and he looked up at the sky quickly, as if to see if the sun had just come from behind a cloud, for so bright was her countenance before him.

"Will your folks let you know when they get home?" Grace asked, knowing that Simon would be concerned until he heard from them.

"Yes. My father said he'd wire us when they get off the train, and Mother promised to write in a day or so. It sure was good to have them here. Even if my mother did put you on the spot with hinting around about wanting grandchildren."

"Your mama is a real sweetheart, Simon. She didn't bother me one little bit. I can't wait to have your babies."

"Do you mean that, Grace? You won't mind if you are in a family way right off?"

"First we'll have to be intimate, Simon, before I can think about babies."

"Well, maybe in a couple of months or so, now that I think about it," Simon said, not wanting to rush Grace into motherhood before she was ready for it. "We need to settle in with each other before we have a third member in this family," he said, smiling at her.

His lips curved in a smile as he busied himself with opening the gate in front of the parsonage. "I thought we'd settled in pretty good last night, love. I feel almost like a husband already, and you look just like a wife ought to, pretty and shiny, kinda like a brand-new penny."

She frowned at him mockingly. "A penny? Is that all I'm worth?"

He shook his head. "Ah, sweetheart, I can't tell you how much you mean to me, how highly I prize you. I won't even try, for you wouldn't believe me."

"Give it a try, Mr. Grafton. You've talked yourself into a hole. Now just try to get out of it."

The front door swung open at his touch and he escorted her into the house, halting her in the hallway, bending low to whisper against her ear.

"I didn't frighten you too badly, Grace, did I? On our wedding night and then again last night?"

"Last night?" She looked up at him in surprise. "Last night we just slept in the middle of the bed. You didn't even... Well, you know, we didn't..."

He took pity on her. "You know why, honey. I didn't want to hurt you and I knew you were upset. I'll do better in a day or so. Perhaps you'll let me closer to you tonight. I can only hope so. But I did sleep with my arms around you all night, you know. I sure didn't give you room to get away from me. But I knew by the way you looked that you weren't ready yet for my loving."

She dropped her face against his chest. "I will be, Simon," she whispered softly. And then she looked up at him and her smile was perfection to his eyes. "I'll try ever so hard to be your wife tonight," she said, leaning against him, as if she craved his touch on her body.

Simon ran his palms down her sides, from beneath her arms to her hips, and then encircled her with arms that promised much, and hands that offered her pleasure.

She faced him, nestling closely to him, her head on his shoulder. "I promise you I'll try to make you happy tonight, Simon. I'll really try to be what you want."

"You already are, Grace. And if we don't consummate our marriage tonight, it will be another night, but it must be when you're ready. I promise not to rush you again."

Grace looped her index finger through Simon's watch chain, which reached from one side of his vest to the other. "See how long we have until it's time to begin dinner, Simon. I'll have to give Ethel a hand with preparations."

He obliged her, pulling his watch from the pocket designed to hold it and showing her the time. "It's only eleven now, Grace. Ethel won't care if you don't help with today's dinner, anyway."

"Well, I care," she said. "You go spend some time in the yard, Simon. I have things to do, now that I'm a wife." He smiled, nodding his approval of her as she escaped to the kitchen where she heard Ethel puttering about.

They walked through town after supper that evening, a slow stroll that once more exposed them to the neighbors who watched from porches and called out to them. Simon was popular in town, Grace had decided, for the men seemed to enjoy his company and the women cast her looks of… perhaps *envy* was too strong a word for the expression on their faces when the younger females of the town spied their handsome minister out and about.

Grace only knew that she was proud to be his wife and the overflow of interest in Simon fell on her. Folks were friendly to her, the ladies including her in their conversations after church, the menfolk polite and courteous. She'd done well to marry Simon, for she'd found a place in the community, if only by association with him.

Simon opened the front door and they went into the house, a single lamp in the parlor to light their way. Grace sat down on the sofa and Simon found his place beside her. From the kitchen a kettle or pan rattled against the stove and Ethel could be heard humming softly.

"Are you ready for bed, Grace? Or do you want a piece of the pie Ethel made for dessert first? I'm sure there were several pieces left over if you'd like a cup of tea and another piece of pie," Simon told her.

"No, I think I'm ready for bed," she said, a flush

rising to cover her cheeks, perhaps at the thought of her promise to him.

Simon rose and held out his hand to her, then led her across the parlor and into the foyer. He called out to Ethel as they reached the foot of the stairway. "We're home, Ethel and we're going up to bed now."

Ethel appeared in the kitchen doorway. "I'm just filling the coffeepot for morning and I'm going to put some wood in the stove and bank it for the night. I'll be up in a few minutes."

"Good night, Ethel," Grace said.

"You sleep tight, Grace. Morning comes early."

They headed up the stairs, Simon's arm around her waist, holding her close. He opened the bedroom door, and Grace crossed the threshold and took her nightgown from beneath her pillow.

Simon sat on the edge of the bed, removing his shoes and stockings, then rising to strip off his vest and shirt, tossing his tie over the back of a chair, lest it be wrinkled up on the floor with the rest of his clothing. He scooped up his drawers and tossed them into the laundry basket, then sat on the bed, the sheet pulled up over his lap, both pillows behind him as he awaited Grace's appearance from behind the screen where she'd gone to undress.

She wasn't long, a matter of a few minutes, and his eyes lit with desire as she approached the bed.

"Did you leave me any room, Simon? I see you've confiscated my pillow. Where am I supposed to put my head?"

He patted his bare chest and grinned. "Right here, sweetheart. I'll scoot down in bed and if you'll just come lie down and put your head right here, I'll rub your back and we can talk for a bit."

She slid beneath the sheet and quilt and scooted close to him, accepting his arm around her and the hand that guided her head to rest against his shoulder. Even from there, his heartbeat sounded against her ear and she thought it a bit rapid. Simon was apparently anxious to make this their wedding night.

As if he knew her thoughts, he slid her from himself until she lay flat on the bed and then lifted her a bit to place her pillow under her head. "Is that better?" he asked.

"It will be when you blow out the candle," she told him, nudging him toward the bedside table where a candle glowed, lighting the room.

"You want the candle out," he said and sighed deeply, as if he rued her words. But he turned his head and blew the flame into oblivion, so that the only light came from the moon and a multitude of stars that shone through the bedroom window.

He hovered over her then, his lips touching the line of her cheek, detouring to capture the lobe of her ear in his mouth for a moment. She shivered as he blew softly into her ear and smothered his laugh against her throat. His kisses were warm against her face, covering her from brow to throat with caresses she cherished, even as his hands were warm against her, his fingers against her bodice, unbuttoning her gown.

She offered no protest, for she'd known he would want to see her breasts without covering again. For some reason, he was drawn to those curves and she felt a shred of pride envelop her that this man was so pleased to touch her and hold her, admire her and shed his kisses on her flesh.

His head bent and he did just that, kissing his way from her collarbone down to the soft curve of her breast, his tongue touching her skin, his teeth gentle in their touch against the pink nubbin of flesh that he seemed so drawn to. She shivered as he ran his tongue over that bit of skin that hardened at his touch, that drew up into a beggar aching for his caress once more.

And he obliged, as if he knew that she was not averse to his handling of her breasts. He reached for the hem of her nightgown and tugged at it, loosening it from beneath her until he was able to uncover her body. She lay acquiescent beneath his touch, hearing his soft whispers, reaching to touch his face and smooth his hair.

Things were progressing nicely, Simon decided, even though he was operating in the dark here.

His hands moved slowly against her warm flesh, one finger touching the hollow of her navel, then sliding down a bit to touch the soft triangle of hair that curled low on her belly. He ruffled it a bit, feeling her shiver and hearing her soft laughter as she responded to his fingers touching her there in that secret place where no man had ever trespassed.

He felt a bit braver, for she had not halted his exploration, but seemed to be willing to allow him his way in this. Her sigh was soft against his face as his hand slid between her thighs, as if he warmed his fingers there where her skin was tender, her flesh fragile. His head bent to her once more and his kisses were spread from temple to cheek, then to her mouth where he spent long minutes persuading her to his will. With success it seemed, for she joined in his play, her own hands against the thatch of hair on his chest, her fingertips caressing the small male nipples, then moving to surround him with her touch, her arms circling him, her hands against his back now.

Desire filled him to overflowing, his passion rising as he spent his caresses against her skin. His tongue laved the tender skin of her throat, from there to her breasts, tasting of the sweetness she did not deny him. His mind spun with the pleasure she offered so unstintingly, and the joy of discovery filled him.

Still her arms encircled him, her fingers reaching

again to bury themselves in his hair and she murmured her pleasure at his touch. "I didn't know
that would feel so good, Simon," she whispered
and he groaned, a sound of pleasure he made no
attempt to withhold, his mouth opening to suckle
her breasts. She wiggled beneath him and her legs
captured his hand, holding it there against the heat
of a woman's needy flesh.

"Grace, open your legs for me. I want to touch
you and you've taken my hand captive." He swallowed the laughter that begged to be released, and
buried his face in the valley between her breasts,
lest she take offense at his chuckles.

But her own laughter was smothered by a hand
she pressed against her lips. She obeyed his urgent
need, her legs relaxing at his words, her knees
parting and lifting, opening to him, offering him
admittance to the feminine place where no man had
known of her softness, the tender folds of womanhood that were offered now to her husband.

He was touched by her trust, stunned by the
warmth of her embrace as arms enclosed him,
hands caressed him and fingers tested the strong
muscles of his back and then slid to his chest. She
showed no fear, no hesitation. When his touch
became more demanding against her, when his
hands knew her as a husband knows a wife, she
inhaled sharply, but relaxed in mere moments,

only kissing the flesh of his chest, for her face was buried there.

"Simon." Again she spoke his name in a whisper, and now there was joy in the syllables she spoke, pleasure expressed by the touch of her lips, her hands and the brush of her body lifting against his as she sought and found the sheer delight his agile fingers promised. She was like fire against him, burning with the flames of desire as she claimed the pleasure he brought to her with the touch of his hand.

He moved then, opening her legs farther so that he might lie close to the warmth of her woman's flesh. She was damp, shivering in his embrace, and he petted her gently, letting her know he would not rush this part of their loving, whispering sounds that spoke of his need for her, his unwillingness to hurt her in any way. And then he tenderly, carefully fit their bodies together, aching to thrust within her, yet able to find his way gently, for he yearned to bring her pleasure to exceed that which she'd already claimed as her own.

And in all of that, he succeeded, for she flinched but a moment as he broke the barrier within and found the haven he'd sought.

"Grace?" His voice was soft against her ear, his words hesitant. "Are you all right? I'm sorry, sweetheart. I know I hurt you, but it will never cause you pain again. I promise."

And she shook her head, a quick movement he could not fail to see and feel against himself, and her words were joyous, unstained by any pain or fear. "Oh, no, Simon. It was only for a moment. You didn't hurt me."

He withdrew only a bit, and then pushed farther into her, feeling the taut flesh give way before his taking, and she drew her knees up, as if to grip him firmly and hold him in place.

"Ah, Grace. Just like that, sweetheart. Hold me tight, Grace." And she did as he asked, as his body encouraged her to respond. And then he recognized the sound of her breathing as it changed once more, became more hurried, and she again found the pleasure his body could provide her.

Her sigh was sweet, her embrace one of passion and desire, and he bent to touch her throat with his tongue, his lips and finally with the edge of his teeth, knowing she would wear his mark on the morrow. That she would find a small spot on her throat, there where her dress would cover it when it was buttoned.

And he knew she would be aware of that mark throughout the day when she looked at him, when their eyes met over the breakfast table, when the afternoon gave way to evening and night was upon them once more. For it was a mark of his possession and she was his bride.

Chapter Ten

She awoke with a start, feeling a warm hand on her belly, against her bare skin. Simon lay beside her and his chuckle was almost silent. "I knew that would wake you up, sweetheart. You're not used to finding a man's hands on you."

Grace turned her head to see him grinning at her. "I think you're taking advantage of me, Mr. Grafton."

"No, just admiring my beautiful bride a bit. I suspect it's time to get up, for I smell the coffee from the kitchen, but I was just enjoying watching you wake up. You're a beautiful woman in the morning, Grace. Especially *this* morning."

She lifted her hand to his face, her fingers cradling his cheek. "How about in the afternoon and evening?"

"I'll let you know later on, when I've taken you to bed tonight. When I get a chance to see your blue eyes in the candlelight. For I don't intend to blow it out tonight."

"You'll want to do…do *that* in a room all lit up with a candle?"

Simon smothered a laugh against her throat, bending to kiss her where her pulse beat in a hectic manner. "A candle doesn't cast a whole lot of light, love. And I want to see you when I touch you and hear you make those soft sounds of pleasure like you did last night. And afterward, when I lie beside you on the bed, will you open your eyes? Better yet, will you open them and look at me when I'm making love to you, sweetheart? I want to watch your eyes turn dark when you feel my body against yours."

"How do you know they'll turn dark? And what does that mean, anyway?"

"I saw them in the moonlight last night. Your face was touched by a moonbeam coming through the window, and when we came together as one, you opened them wide and then they looked somehow darker. As if you felt something more, more than just me being close to you, being inside of you. I can't explain it any better than that."

"It was like we were no longer separate, like I was truly a part of you then, Simon. Like our bodies were joined in more than just a physical sense, perhaps as though our souls were making love, as well."

He agreed. "And that's the difference in married love, when two people are pledged, each to the other. Between that and the sort of thing that drives men to such places as Belle's room above the saloon."

"Maybe Belle doesn't know any different. Maybe she's to be pitied," Grace said quietly, thinking once more of her own blessings, and the unfortunate woman who had met up with tragedy.

"We all make choices, Grace. You've chosen to be a woman of strength. A woman willing to be married and support your husband in every way. You can't deny that, can you?"

She shook her head, thinking of the choices she might have made in her life. "When I recognize the sort of young men who wanted to court me back home, for what they expected of me, it almost frightens me. For I could have made a terrible mistake by accepting their attentions, perhaps marrying one of them. And then where would I be?"

"Well, not here with me," Simon said, reminding her of her vulnerability.

"And do you think I'd trade places with anyone else in the world?" she asked, reaching up to him, her fingers touching his cheek, brushing the hair from his brow.

His mouth hovered over hers for a moment and

then his words were rasped in her ear, and she shivered with delight.

"Trade places? Hah! You don't stand a chance, lady. You don't stand a chance."

The days seemed to fly by in the parsonage, Grace settling in as if she'd been born for it, and Simon with his head in the clouds, finding it difficult to concentrate on his daily tasks. He managed to visit several of his members who were not feeling well, including Belle, who, though not one of the congregation, still needed any comfort he could bring.

Grace went with him on that visit. They walked up the stairs to where the singers, dancers and barmaids slept, each in their own room, and Grace tried not to think of what sort of business was carried on there.

"I shouldn't have brought you along, sweetheart. I know you're not comfortable with this," Simon said, as he knocked on Belle's door.

"Well, maybe she'd like to talk to another woman, Simon. I'm not so straitlaced that I can't understand a little bit about her life."

He frowned down at her. "You have no idea, sweetheart. None at all." And with that, a woman's voice called out for her visitors to enter.

Simon opened the door and escorted Grace into the room. "It's Reverend Grafton, Belle. And this is my wife, Grace," he said quietly, urging Grace into the room.

"I noticed you at the wedding and appreciated your presence there," Grace said. "I thought it was a beautiful service and a beautiful day I'll always remember."

A lovely woman, or at least a woman who would one day again be lovely, sat on a chair in the room, her face still bruised, the bruises looking too familiar to Grace, for they almost matched the ones she'd seen in her own mirror not so long ago. One arm was wrapped with a splint and tied across her chest for support, and Belle did not attempt to rise to her feet to greet them.

"I'm sure you'll forgive me for remaining in my chair," she said.

"I thought, or perhaps hoped, you'd be feeling a bit better by now," Simon said, reaching to take her hand in his.

"I'm much better, Mr. Grafton. Just can't move my face much. It hurts to open my eyes very far or even to talk. I think I had several teeth loosened. One thing's for sure. I sure am sick of soup. I wore my heaviest veil to your wedding, so as not to be too conspicuous."

Grace moved to crouch before her, taking one of the woman's hands in her own. "You needn't talk if you don't want to, Belle. Simon and I just wanted to let you know we're thinking of you and

I wanted to come along today and see if I could do anything to lend a hand." Grace felt helpless in the face of Belle's injuries and then decided she might be accepted more by the woman if she confided her own problems.

"I was in almost the same shape as you are a while back, Belle. I was set upon and bruised up. I remember well how sore I was, how miserable I felt. So I have some idea of how helpless you feel, not able to do much but sit there and hurt."

"You're the girl that the Summers fella hurt, aren't you?" Belle asked, peering through an eye still swollen and bruised.

"I'm the one," Grace admitted. "The only difference is that I was rescued before he could hurt me as badly as he hurt you."

She looked up at Simon and her eyes shone with joy as she spoke his name. "Simon, here..." She bit her lip and almost stammered, so strongly did he affect her as she remembered the day he'd first seen her. "Well, Simon not only rescued me, he took good care of me, Belle."

"It was a lovely wedding. And you were a beautiful bride," Belle said, releasing Simon's hand to clasp Grace's tightly in her own.

"She was," Simon told Belle. "Still is, to tell the truth."

"You've got that right, mister. You're a lucky

fella. Grace is pretty as a picture. It's no wonder you snatched her up in a hurry."

Simon brought a second chair for Grace to sit upon and she leaned closer to Belle. "Can I help you in any way, ma'am? I can sew or cook or even take you home with me if needs be and look after you for a while."

Simon thought he would choke when Grace's words penetrated his brain. She had offered the parsonage to a woman who was…well, who was a soiled dove, as his mother would have said. And yet, his own mother would have done the same, he realized, understanding that women seemed to form a closed society when it came to such things. And as a man, he must only stand on the outside and be an observer. But Belle, whether she understood his unspoken dilemma or preferred her own surroundings, set his mind at ease.

"Thanks, Grace. I sure appreciate your offer, but the girls here are taking care of me. If you'd like to stop by again with your husband, I'd appreciate it. I don't have a lot of company."

"I can't help it, Simon. I feel sorry for her. I know she's just a saloon girl, but for all that, she has a mother somewhere who probably loves her and would feel terrible if she knew what had happened to Belle."

Not likely. But Simon was wise enough not to

spew out his opinion, and simply squeezed Grace's hand as they walked back to the parsonage. The sheriff hailed them from the doorway of his office and they halted to speak.

"Been out visiting?" he asked Simon.

"Just making a call. Grace went along to keep me company."

"Didn't I just see the two of you going into the saloon an hour or so ago?"

"We spent some time with Miss Belle. Grace wanted to see if she could do anything to offer help of any sort." And then, thinking of Grace's offer, Simon grinned. "She almost got us in a peck of trouble, Charlie."

"I did not," Grace said vehemently. "I only asked the woman if she wanted to come to the parsonage to recuperate."

Charlie covered his eyes with one hand. "Oh, my. You are a wonder, Miss Grace. I've heard of innocent women, but you take the cake."

"Now, Charlie, innocence is all right. It's just that Grace has a heart bigger than all outdoors and she hated to see Belle in such shape."

Grace shot him a look that promised retribution later on and Simon wisely changed the subject.

"Just wanted you to know what was going on," he said, refusing to meet the lawman's eye as he spoke. "If there's anything else happening, we'll stop by."

"Well, I have the note and that bundle of weeds to show the judge, and that should be enough to make him aware of what's gone on," Charlie said.

"Why don't you come by the house at supper time, Sheriff?" Grace asked. "We'd enjoy having you share our meal with us. And Ethel always cooks plenty."

And so it was that the sheriff stayed for supper, eating Mrs. Anderson's cooking and listening to her lighten the conversation with stories of her daughter and the children she'd visited for several days.

It was dark before Charlie Wilson left, and he shook Simon's hand, uttering a few words of warning as he stepped across the threshold, cautioning the younger man to be on the alert for trouble.

"As if I'd let you out of my sight," Simon told Grace, leading her down the hallway to their room.

"Well, your housekeeper feels the same way. She's very protective of us, Simon. We're lucky to have her."

Simon opened the bedroom door and entered ahead of Grace, looking around quickly, opening the wardrobe and checking behind the screen before he shut the door.

"I think the ladies are plotting against you, Grace," he said with a grin.

"What ladies? The ladies at church?" she asked, stunned by his words.

"Yes, the ladies at church. I heard a rumor that they're about to ask you to be in charge of the flowers for the altar every week, since we have the nicest flower garden in town." His grin was wide as he faced her, pulling her to her feet and working at her buttons.

"And that isn't all there is to it. They seem to think you might like to be in charge of the women's quilting for the orphanage in Wallen's Creek, over in the next county. They've committed themselves to making a half dozen or so quilts a year and they want to be sure you have enough to do to keep you busy."

"As if keeping you happy isn't enough for me to attend to," she said, her chin lowering, allowing her to peer down at her waist as she watched his hands untying the tapes that held her petticoats up.

"Oh, you're doing a fine job of that," he told her. "You haven't heard me complain, have you?"

She shot him a look over her shoulder. "I would hope not."

"You don't have any worries there," he said, beginning to work on her drawers, his fingers agile as he managed to lower them right behind the petticoats. And then he looked up over her shoulder, as if something had caught his eye, and his hands pushed her down on the bed, snatching up the sheet and drawing it over her shoulders.

Grace cried out and watched in astonishment as he went to the window and bent to look outdoors. With a soft mumbled word she could not decipher, he locked the sash and then pulled the curtains closed over the glass panes, the fabric dense enough to protect their privacy.

"What's wrong?" she asked, pulling the quilt up to cover herself.

"There was someone out there. I saw a shadow though the glass, but they disappeared before I could see who it was."

"More than one person?" she asked. "Maybe Ethel was out in the yard. She's been feeding a stray cat sometimes at night."

"It wasn't a woman," Simon said firmly.

He crossed the room to where she sat, the quilt half around her shoulders, her breasts exposed to his view. *If anyone had seen her...* He gritted his teeth, seeing a shiver take her in its grip, and then he sat beside her on the bed.

"It's all right, honey. Probably just one of the young boys in the neighborhood, playing a prank. Or maybe it *was* Ethel. We'll have to ask her in the morning." His arms circled her and he pulled her into his embrace, holding her until she wiggled against him.

"Simon, you're squeezing me half to death." She

pouted her protest against his chest and he laid her back against the pillow, confident that no prying eyes could see within the room now.

"I didn't mean to hurt you, sweetheart. I just didn't want anyone to be looking in our room and it upset me to see something move out there. Probably wasn't anything at all."

And yet, she knew better, for Simon was not easily startled or upset. And now his actions when they'd entered their bedroom made more sense to her. He'd thought someone might have come into the house while they were gone. No one in town ever locked a door, but even as she thought those words, Simon went to their bedroom door and opened it.

"I'm going to set the bolts on the front and back doors, just in case," he said, his smile seeming taut to her eyes. And when he came back in the bedroom, just minutes later, he turned the latch on that door, too.

Grace refused to ask questions, only held out her arms to him, seeming unaware of the picture she presented, there in his bed.

But Simon was more than aware, his gaze captured by the beauty of blue eyes and dark hair against the pristine whiteness of his pillow. She was a prize, a woman above all others to his mind, and he vowed once more to protect her from all peril.

Even as he lowered himself to her side, taking her in his arms, he felt a thread of fear slide down the length of his spine, the knowledge that all was not as it should be, and that his Grace might be in more danger than they'd thought.

She kissed him, as if she were intent on focusing his attention on her, away from the locked doors and drawn curtains. And he could not turn aside, for her sweetness was like honey to his lips, her aroma that of clean woman, perhaps due to a faint scent of the soap she used. And yet, Grace had drawn him, from the first, with her unique being. She had what no other woman of his acquaintance had ever possessed—an aura of femininity that overwhelmed his senses.

And at that thought, he inhaled the scent of rainwater from her hair, for she and Ethel both used the collected water from the barrel at the side of the house to wash their hair. Then as he allowed his face to lie in the bend of her throat, he caught the aroma of clean skin and a woman untouched by powder and paint, with only her own natural beauty to lure the eye.

He held her close, his hands moving on her back, his body already prepared to love her, to take her with him into the world they shared here on this bed.

And Grace was willing, for she responded to him, and he thought it was with an almost frantic need, her mouth opening against his skin, her hands clutching at him as if she feared he might disappear if she did not hold fast.

He tried to halt her, to slow the pace she seemed determined to set, and could not. Not without drawing away from her, and that he would not do. And so, they came together in a flood of emotion, his skin hot and tight as she clung to him. He heard the beating of his heart, filling his chest and thrumming like a hammer pounding an anvil in the blacksmith's shop. The shadows of the night swirled around them, and he welcomed the darkness, for it enclosed them totally, her skin smooth against his hands, her body rising to meet his.

"Grace, I don't want to hurt you," he said tightly, fearful of her not being ready for his possession. But her arms drew him closer, her legs parted to hold him there where she was determined he should be, and he found himself filling her with his masculine need, recognized that she had not been caressed and prepared by him enough to find a satisfaction of her own. She would not allow him to halt the loving of her body, but clung to him with fierce ardor.

He was lost in her arms, the recipient of a torrent of loving, a flood tide of her desire. And it seemed that Grace felt a woman's need that tossed them adrift in a wild stream that could only be crossed by two people together.

Simon held his woman close, for she had loved him well, this young girl, no longer virgin, but yet untried. A wife whose love for the man she held was enough to toss her headlong into a bliss such as she'd not known before this night, for she cried out the syllables of his name as if they were a plea for his kisses and the caresses he spread upon her tender flesh.

Simon felt the strong pulsing of her feminine parts, knew she had found surcease for her searching. And then sought his own ease, whispering soft words against her cheek, his mouth opening against the soft skin of her throat, his heart beating as one with that of the woman he held.

His wife. His love.

The sheriff was in his office the next day as Simon stopped by to tell him of the figure outside the bedroom window. "You think it was a grown man?" Charlie asked, and Simon nodded his agreement.

"I didn't make a fuss over it, just made sure the window was locked and pulled the shade down. I didn't want to upset Grace any more than I had to."

"The judge is due here, and I heard the train stop just a few minutes ago, so he well may be coming down the road any minute," Charlie said, rising and going to the doorway to look outside.

"Good morning," he called out as the man they'd been expecting neared the jailhouse.

Judge Hale spoke a greeting to Charlie and then turned to Simon. "You're the preacher, aren't you?" he asked.

Simon nodded and then listened as Charlie let the magistrate know what had gone on over the past day or so. He brought forth the note from his desk, spoke of the sad-looking bundle of weeds Simon and Grace had found on their porch and then told of Simon's late-night visitor at the parsonage.

"When you add up the injuries to two women and the fella checking out the preacher's house last night, I'd say you've got a peck of trouble, Sheriff. Have you had any more luck in finding the man we're searching for, Charlie? I'd hoped you might have located him by now."

"Not yet. I took a deputy out again last evening and we rode around through the woods where there's been a report of someone having a campfire lately, but we didn't find anything. Some cold ashes, but nothing to make our search worthwhile."

"We need to increase your staff, find a couple more men to deputize until this scoundrel is found, Charlie. The women in this town aren't safe as it stands right now. Especially not the young woman this preacher married. Sounds to me like you've got a madman loose."

Charlie Wilson's brow was furrowed, his mouth

drawn down as he listened to the judge's words. "I couldn't agree with you more, sir, but I'm stumped. And until someone sees the man or finds a trace of him somewhere, our hands are tied. Don't think we've given up, only retrenched, for he *will* be found. And sooner rather than later."

"Well, I'd say this preacher of yours deserves better than that as an answer to the problem, Charlie. Surely you can post a man outside the parsonage, even if only during the night hours. I'll send to St. Louis for a marshal if need be, but the woman… Her name is Grace…am I right?"

At Simon's nod of agreement, Judge Hale continued. "Your wife deserves the protection of the law, and even if that involves taking her into custody—"

"Stop right there." Simon's voice was loud, and then he offered a shrug as if to apologize, backtracking a bit, as if he sensed he'd overstepped with his abrasive behavior. Yet, what less could the judge expect?

So his words were firm, allowing no question from either of the gentlemen before him. "My wife stays with me, and if I have to sleep with a gun beside me, I'll do it. But no one takes her anywhere, not without me following about a foot behind."

Judge Hale grinned. "Well, I'm glad to see you have your priorities straight, young man." He looked pointedly at the jailhouse door then. "And where is your wife this morning?"

Simon felt chagrined at the words, knowing he'd just put his foot in his mouth. "I left her with my housekeeper while I walked over to speak with Charlie. And I get the message, sir. I should have brought her with me."

"If only so I could meet the lady."

"Why don't you take a walk with me right now and I'll introduce you. I'll guarantee there's a piece of apple pie in it for you."

Judge Hale waved his hand, laughing. "I'll get settled in at the hotel first, Reverend. And then you'll see me heading your way. Just point out the place."

"Right next door to the church, down the road to your left when you leave here. A small white house with a green swing on the porch."

And even as he spoke Simon thought of Grace sitting at home awaiting his return, knew a moment of anxiety and took his leave. With a nod of his head, he strode from the office and headed down the road. Suddenly, seeing Grace was the most important thing in the world. And he walked quickly as he made haste to the parsonage.

Chapter Eleven

The front door slammed behind him as he entered the house, and he heard voices from the kitchen.

"Simon, is that you?"

"None other," he called out. "And why wasn't the door locked?" He strode into the kitchen and his eyes swept over the two women at the table. Grace smiled at him and rose to greet him, her hands clasping his, her face lifting for a kiss.

Simon bent to her, his lips touching hers briefly, squeezing her fingers in his and whispering softly, his voice low as he uttered words meant only for her ears, and then spoke aloud the news they'd been awaiting.

"We've got company coming," Simon said, addressing both ladies. "Judge Henry Hale is in town and he'd like to meet my wife."

"Oh, Simon. I'm hardly fit to meet the man who picks up the trash in the road, let alone an important man like the judge." Grace looked down at her dress, one hand smoothing the wrinkled fabric of the skirt as she spoke.

Simon's long fingers touched her chin and caught her attention. "You look just fine, Grace, just as a preacher's wife should. You're all covered, but for your bare feet," he said with a chuckle, looking down at the pink toes that peeked from beneath her skirt.

"I'll get dressed in something nicer, and I'll put my shoes on," she said, turning to the doorway and making haste as she went up the stairs to their bedroom. Simon was right behind her and he thought of what he'd told the judge just minutes ago.

Following Grace was no hardship, he'd decided. Certainly, keeping a close eye on her might claim a good bit of his time, but of that he'd never complain, for he could think of nothing more pleasurable than focusing his attention on his bride.

She quickly slid from her housedress and chose another, a bit newer, from the wardrobe and pulled it over her head, buttoning it swiftly. In moments she was sitting on the edge of the bed and he knelt before her, reaching for her shoes and slipping them into place. Her laugh was sparkling, a far cry from the look of despair she'd worn late last night when she'd sat in this same spot.

And Simon silently vowed to keep her laughter ever present, to lavish his care upon her so fully that she need never fret or stew again over the presence of evil in her life.

It was an hour later and they sat together on the porch, the green swing in motion as Judge Hale entered their gate and sauntered to where they sat. He sat down heavily on the top step and wiped his brow with a white handkerchief drawn from his hip pocket.

"Sure is a hot one today, Preacher. Not a single bit of breeze through my hotel-room window, and not much better out here."

"Would you like a chair to sit on, sir?" Simon asked, for two porch chairs sat against the wall.

"No, this is just fine. I'm in the shade and that's all that matters," the judge said.

"How about a nice glass of lemonade?" Grace asked, rising quickly from the swing.

The man turned to give her his full attention. "I think I'd be more refreshed just looking at you, Mrs. Grafton."

He extended his hand and Grace took it between both of hers, greeting him with a smile of genuine welcome. "Simon told me you were coming by to visit for a bit. I'm sorry you were called to town for such a terrible reason, but nonetheless, I'm pleased to meet you, sir."

His eyes were admiring as he smiled up at Grace

and she withdrew her hand from his to take her leave. "I'll be right back with some lemonade for both of you," she said, pulling open the screen door and entering the house.

Simon heard her footsteps in the foyer, heard the faint brush of her slippers on the bare floor and then the sound of voices from the kitchen.

"She's a lovely lady, sir," Judge Hale said quietly. "Definitely worth any sacrifice you make to keep her safe. I'd be tempted to put her in a safe place and bolt all the doors until her tormentor is found."

"I've tried to make that safe place her home, Judge Hale. For the man we seek is not only her tormentor, but a brute who is capable of hateful actions. I fear we've seen his work demonstrated here in town over the past days, and our women live in fear. As to my wife, I have pledged myself to watch over her, even to the extent of carrying a sidearm and having one nearby in our bedroom at night. I brought a rifle to town with me when I arrived months ago, and it has accompanied me on my outings when I travel from home to call on my parishioners. But as far as my handgun is concerned, it won't be far from my reach now, until this is cleared up."

"I can't blame you. And I assure you here and now that should the culprit be killed during his capture, no man will ever be arrested for any part in his death."

"I sincerely hope it is not myself, sir. For I find it difficult to live with the idea of killing another human being. I put a shot in his shoulder the first time I saw him and grieved over my actions, even though I knew I had no choice and indeed would have been praised had he succumbed to the wound. Even my bishop told me I should bear no shame at my behavior that day, but my dedication to the God I serve has brought many an hour of doubt to my mind as to my qualifications."

"I think you need not doubt your faith, Preacher, but rather put your support behind any means used to find this man."

"That I will do," Simon said, as he thought of the woman he'd married and the great peril he may have brought to her life—and his own—with that single action. For Kenny's pursuit of Grace, his determination that she marry him, had made Simon aware that the man might well harbor hatred toward the man she'd chosen to marry.

The screen door opened and he rose quickly as Grace backed from the doorway, holding a tray with three glasses on it, along with a pitcher of lemonade, two slices of apple pie and a small platter of cookies.

"The cookies are just out of the oven, and Mrs. Anderson sends her best wishes, along with the apple pie, sir." Her smile added value to the offering she carried and Simon thought he'd never been so proud of her, for she was obviously determined to present the picture of a good hostess, no matter the circumstances.

The pie had disappeared and the plate of cookies was a smattering of crumbs by the time the judge left. He bowed to Grace, and Simon's farewell to the gentleman was sincere.

"I can't tell you how much I appreciate your coming to town and supporting our sheriff in this, sir. I'm grateful for your help."

The two men shook hands and Judge Hale remarked quietly on the faint evidence of bruising he'd noticed on Grace's face. "Seems to me that the man was sure enough violent, when she still bears proof of her injuries at his hand."

"He struck her with his closed fist, as he might have hit another man," Simon told him. "She was a sight to see for the first week or so."

The judge shook his head in silent commiseration, then offered his hand to Simon. "I'm pleased that her life has been made happier, and I'd say you're the fella who made it all happen," he said with a smile.

"It was my pleasure," Simon told him as the judge walked through the gate and headed down the road toward the hotel. Simon turned back to the porch and escorted Grace into the house, catching a scent of supper cooking as they entered the hallway.

"I can't say that I'm very hungry. I fear I over-ate on the cookies," he told her, drawing her to the parlor, sitting beside her on the sofa.

She turned to him and as if by some form of magic, her smile disappeared, her eyes filled with tears and she slumped dejectedly beside him, her hands gripped tightly in her lap. "What will we do, Simon? We can't live in fear much longer, for it is eating me alive today. I have to wonder if there's any way to draw Mr. Summers out and face him down."

"Certainly not by you, Grace. You'll not even consider putting yourself in peril in such a way."

She lifted her chin and he thought she looked as though she'd taken on strength from some inner source. "If it will keep one more woman safe or another girl like myself from harm, then it will be worth any risk. If I had not been the object of Kenny Summers's attention in the first place, none of this would have happened. I feel… responsible."

Simon shook his head at her words, his voice overriding her soft tones as he denied her avowal of guilt. "You were only in the wrong place, Grace. Kenny chose his own path, and you had no part in the evil things he's done."

"And yet, he's done things because of me, Simon,

and you can't deny that. Ethel wouldn't have been shot at had I not been here in this house. I won't claim blame for his other doings because I don't think I could bear being the pivot upon which his evil actions have rotated. But I know that I'll do whatever I can to bring him to justice."

"You'll stay in this house behind locked doors and remain safe, is what you'll do, Grace. I won't have it any other way."

"Simon, we spoke of something similar on another day when you said I must not feel compelled to obey you as if you were my parent. I promised to love and honor you. It was your choice to leave the word *obey* out of our marriage. You can't change that now."

He was stunned, almost to the point of being speechless, for his wife had never stated her thoughts so bluntly before now. And for a long moment, he rued the day he'd drawn a firm line through the missing word in their vows. And yet, he would not have Grace following him blindly, for she was too intelligent for him to expect that sort of behavior from her. But in this one thing, he felt justified in taking a stand. And if it meant the difference between her living or facing unknown peril, he *would* take a stand.

"I won't have it, Grace. This is where I draw the line." If he noticed the color leave her face, if her eyes seemed stark and lifeless, it made no difference to what he'd determined and he continued.

"You will be in a safe place at all times. I don't want you alone, and if it is not possible or seemly for you to accompany me in my daily doings, then I will expect to find you behind locked doors when I return to you."

She was silent, her head bowed now as if she could not bear to meet his gaze, and he saw two salty drops fall to stain the bodice of her dress. But Grace was nothing if not proud and determined. And so she stood, and looking over his head toward the window where the sun was setting, she spoke in a voice that was chilled and steady.

"I will do as you say, so long as it is not to another's disadvantage. By that I mean that should I feel compelled to leave this house to aid another, or should I decide to make a move you might not approve of, this conversation is null and void."

"That isn't the way it works. You will obey me in this or I'll take the recommendation of the law in this town and have you put into protective custody."

His heart ached for her as she trembled before him, for never had he thought to threaten her in such a way, and yet he could not allow her to put herself in peril.

"And does that mean I'll be in a jail cell? Where any person so inclined can peer at me through the

bars or through the window to the out of doors?"
Her gaze shifted then and he was struck by the
dark chill of those blue eyes.

"If you are put into protective custody it might
mean being in a cell, but certainly no one would be
allowed anywhere near it, and no one would have
access but myself and the sheriff. Although I think
the phrase might also mean being in the safety of
your own home with a person in attendance at all
times to protect you."

"A prisoner in my own home? What difference
is that from being locked in a jail cell? And how
can you endorse such a thing and still call me
your beloved? Which, if I remember rightly, you
used as a term of endearment just last night. Of
course, it wasn't said in anyone else's hearing, or
even aloud, now that I think about it, so perhaps it
doesn't count."

Pain such as he'd never felt struck him a blow
midchest, as though she had stabbed him with her
words. And he recalled, vividly, the moment when
he'd whispered the word in her ear, when his heart
had seemed to swell with the knowledge of her
moment of surrender to him in their bed.

He could almost feel the strands of her hair
against his lips, could almost catch a trace of her
scent, almost feel the quiver of response as he'd
whispered the single word of endearment to her.

"Beloved."

* * *

They went to bed as separately as two people could, without the strong bond that had hitherto held them within the boundaries of that mattress, beneath the sheet and within touching distance all throughout the night.

Grace lay quietly at the edge of her side of the bed, almost clinging to the binding edge of the mattress, her back turned to her husband, her eyes tearless but aching. Simon yearned desperately for her, unable to rest, certainly unable to sleep and yet unwilling to back down from the stance he'd taken.

No matter the cost, he would keep her safe. Should she be angry with him, he would strive to overcome the black mood that beset her. Should she defy his edicts and attempt to leave the house without his company, he would lock her in the bedroom. And if by any chance she should escape his limits, he would have her put in a jail cell and protected in whatever way the sheriff deemed right and proper.

He lay in silence, watching the faint movement of her body as she offered him her back, as if unwilling to even allow him a glimpse of her face. And it was too much, too harsh a punishment to bear, all because he wanted to keep her from harm.

He reached for her, turning her with a quick

movement of his hand against her shoulder and she did not fight off his touch, but rolled to her back and for just a single moment, he hoped she had softened toward him, that she had made peace with the words of admonishment he'd spoken.

But it was for naught, for her eyes closed as if she could not bear to look upon him and she turned to her side, facing him, curled into a small, tight being with no degree of leniency toward him. He lifted over her, his hand against her cheek, and spoke softly in the darkness.

"Grace, look at me. Please don't shut me out."

And for just a moment her head turned on the pillow, those blue eyes opened, the heavy lids lifting to expose a gaze so fixed with sorrow, he could hardly bear to focus upon it. And yet, he must try, must offer words that might bend her toward him.

"I never thought to have you look at me so, sweetheart. I only want you safe. I want to raise a family with you and live a long life beside you. I would do you no harm, cause you no pain."

She spoke not a word, only closed her eyes and shut him out, her lips parting for a second as though she would respond, and then as if she possessed library paste between those soft, lush lips, they formed a seamless, single line, and he felt the helpless despair of a man who has chosen a path not to his liking, but sees no other route open to him.

He bent to her and kissed her, for the first time feeling no response from lips that had offered pleasure to him over the past weeks. His hand touched her gown, the one he'd given her on their wedding night, and her body was as still as marble beneath the flesh of his palm.

His fingers curled against the curve of her breast and he drew in a breath that held the faint trace of her own unique aroma, a scent he felt he could exist upon, should nothing else be available to sustain his strength. And again he kissed her, his mouth open against hers, his tongue careful and gentle as he pressed the seam of her lips.

She only caught her breath, for he felt the slight movement as her lips parted just for a second and then closed again. But he'd had a single taste of the woman beneath him, known the flavor of her mouth and would not be denied.

"Will you fight me, Grace? If I take what I need from you, will you push me from you or strike at me in anger?"

Her eyes opened and she spoke then. "You may do as you please, Simon, for I am not as strong as you, and if you want my body, it is yours by law. I have no choice but to do as you ask."

He felt her move beneath him, knew the movement of her legs as she opened them, providing him shelter there where he would have sought his pleasure and her own. Her hands pulled at her gown, tugging it upward until it lay across her waist, leaving her lower body without cover. And he was shamed, his male needs reduced to nothing when he realized she would make a sham of their loving.

His hands pulled her gown back into place, and then his fingers petted the soft curve of her breast, for he could not bear to simply roll over and leave her with pain that made her less than a woman. She'd become unlike his bride in those moments, a *thing,* a vessel for his lust, and he would not accept such painful degradation from her.

And so he bent low again and his mouth was asking a response, seeking a softness she would not offer, as he touched the line of her cheek, tasted the sweet skin at her temple and then brushed the fine tresses of hair from her face, his hand forming against her head, his fingers tingling from the waves and curls that clung to his flesh.

"I hadn't thought to tell you in this way, Grace, but I need to make you understand my great need for you. Not as a body to be used, but as a woman to be cherished. I love you, sweetheart. If you believe nothing else, believe that."

She turned her head from him and he released her, watching as she turned once more to face the window, where the curtains were open, the sash pushed upward. For outside, in the shadows of the bushes, sat a guard pledged to watch that window throughout the night hours. And if he felt that his very soul was on display, Simon cared little, for even had the guard outside the house heard his words, he would not have cared.

For tonight, he only cared about the girl he'd married, to whom he'd just now pledged his love. Not as a part of a wedding ceremony, but as a vow, freely given, yet not accepted.

Her shoulders trembled as he watched, and he heard a faint sound, perhaps a sob, perhaps just the rustle of the sheet as she pulled it over her shoulder. He feared touching her again, lest his need outweigh his good sense. He would not use seduction as a weapon, for if she gave him her body, it must be as before. A gift, a vow unspoken, but alive nevertheless, the opening of herself to his manhood.

And he waited in vain, should she bend, turn to him, even reach back and touch his hand. For any response from her would be an encouragement he would cherish. And then it came, the touch of a small foot against his leg, the movement of toes that settled against his calf muscles.

"Good night, Simon." The words were not what he longed to hear, but they broke the silence between them and he could not fault her. And so his hand lifted to her waist, his palm lay in the hollow between breast and hip, and he felt the warmth of her body begin to melt the chill of his own.

"Good night, Grace. We won't speak of this tomorrow, but know that I love you. Know that I only want what is right for you."

Her foot moved, just an inch or so, but it was answer enough for now, and he opened his hand fully against her soft flesh, knowing she had offered him a tentative olive branch, one he would take gladly.

And so they slept.

Simon was gone when she awoke, and Grace rued for a moment the fact that she could not turn to him and feel his strength beside her. But he'd left the bed early, for the space where he'd been was cool, his pillow still holding the scent of his hair pomade and the faint pine smell of his shaving cream. He'd used it last night before bed, perhaps in hope that she would want his face against hers.

And at that she remembered just such a thing happening, when he'd turned her to him and his skin had touched hers, his hand had been warm on her breast through the fine fabric of her gown. For a moment she felt self-satisfied that she'd offered to accommodate him, pulling her gown up her body and letting him know she was available to him, should he desire to take her.

And then felt shame wash over her being, that she had done such a thing, had offered herself as might a lady above the saloon. For she was a wife, not a *whore*. And that word burned in her mind as if she had spoken it aloud. Certainly it was suitable for such a woman as Belle, and yet, she'd said herself that Belle was to be pitied, not censured.

And so was she, also, Grace Grafton, wife of the minister of the local church, a woman who thought no more of herself than to offer her body in such a way.

He must think her brazen, a creature beyond the respect of a good man, and she was shamed that she had not offered him the abundance of loving he craved. But only the show of an appeasement to his need.

She rose and washed behind the screen, noting that he had closed and locked the sash on the window upon arising. And so she felt safe as she dressed, even as she stood naked for a moment before donning clean undergarments and then a dress from the drawer. She touched the fabric with fingers that appreciated the fine seams, the pearl buttons, the deep hem and the efforts of Ethel, who had shared the sewing of it with her, taking long hours in the doing. The two women would sit together, speaking of nothing but household matters, Grace listening as Ethel spoke of her family and the deep love she held for them.

"Thank you, Ethel," she whispered, her fingers nimble as she slid the buttons into their proper places and brushed the skirt around her hips. And remembered as she did so that Simon had provided the material from the general store for this piece of apparel. Her heart lifted as she thought of him picking and choosing the right colors for her to wear.

"Simon." She whispered his name, sorrow for the pain she'd caused him uppermost in her mind, for she knew her words had stung, her tone had brought an ache to his heart, and she grieved, regretting for a moment the night hours when she might have lain in his arms and had instead chosen to lie as far from him as the bed would allow.

Ethel had made a pot of tea and it sat on the table, still warm enough to drink, accompanied by berries from the garden, picked fresh this morning if Grace was any judge. For even now, she could see that lady bent over the raspberry bushes collecting the bounty they provided.

She'd obviously washed and sugared the first of the day's crop, leaving them for Grace should she arise while the rest of the produce was picked. And Grace ate them with gratitude, reminding herself to thank Simon's housekeeper later on.

A shadow at the back of the garden caught her eye as she swallowed tea, there where the trees provided shade just beyond the berry patch, and even as she watched, Grace saw the form of a man rise and step toward the woman who worked, unaware of the intruder who stole her privacy and infringed upon her work.

"Kenny." It was a harsh whisper from her lips, preceded by a howl of anguish as she rose from the table, her chair falling to the floor, leaving her space to fly on swift feet toward the back door.

"Kenny, don't dare touch her." It was a shriek of warning, words of alarm that brought the house-keeper erect, her body turning as she faced the peril that threatened her. She threw the panful of berries in a single, swooping movement as she used the only weapon she had at hand. The edge of the metal bowl caught Kenny in the forehead, caus-ing him to halt for just a moment in his forward momentum.

It was enough for Ethel to make a hasty escape, running through the rows of green beans, almost tripping over the tomato vines and reaching the back porch just as Kenny scaled the back fence and was gone from the garden.

Ethel's eyes, wide with alarm, met Grace's, whose own heart was beating double-time, whose hands were trembling and whose tears were fall-ing in anguish as she thought of what might have happened right before her eyes.

"Grace, I didn't see him," Ethel said, crying the words out as she slammed the door behind herself. "It's broad daylight out there and he came out of nowhere. Thank God you were up and saw him, for I didn't hear a thing."

Grace embraced her, feeling the trembling that assailed the older woman's body, her anger rising at the man who had dared to trespass in such a way.

"You didn't hurt yourself, running that way, did you? We'll go to the church and tell Simon," she said, leading Ethel to the sink, reaching for a dish towel and dampening it so that she might wipe that lady's face of the tears that fell. Beneath the tears was the countenance of an angry woman, her wrath exploding at being accosted in such a supposedly safe place. It was enough to make a saint utter words that would sting the ears and stain the soul.

And Ethel was no saint. If later she remembered the things she'd said, she never admitted it to Grace, but for those few minutes, the lady was filled with righteous anger and spewed forth a series of accusations and promises for revenge such as Grace had never thought to hear from those prim and proper lips.

"I was here to keep an eye on things and look out for you, Grace," she said finally. "Now I have to tell Simon that I failed in my assignment. Except that I did manage to hit him with my metal bowl. I hope I left a good bruise on his forehead."

"You haven't failed in any way. No such thing,"

Grace said fiercely, for she would not have the housekeeper feel guilty for the misdoing of another. "We'll find the sheriff first and tell him what has happened. In fact, we'll go right now. I think even Simon would agree that we'll be safe on the road in front of the house for a few minutes. There are people in buggies and wagons out there going past, I'd venture to say."

They walked to the front door and looked out upon the road before the house. Within their view were three different vehicles bearing folks in or out of town. The two woman made their way down the walkway to the gate and then hurried down to the church, which sat next to the parsonage. They'd barely reached the side door where Simon's office was located when Simon himself opened the door.

"What happened? Why are the pair of you wandering around alone? You should be indoors with the bolts thrown."

In but a few seconds they made him aware of the happenings, and he stood before Grace, his eyes dark with anger as he allowed them to scan her slender form. "Where are your shoes?" he asked finally, as if that were of some major importance.

She waved a hand as if to brush aside the senseless query and he snatched at it as it passed his chest, holding it between his palms, against his heart. A heart that beat so rapidly, she could feel it through his clothing.

"I'm sorry, Simon. We didn't think of anything but notifying the sheriff, and shoes were the last thing from my mind."

He nodded as a buggy slowed and the man driving the mare called out. It was Mr. Aldrich, the president of the bank. He jumped from the buggy seat and approached the three who stood before the parsonage.

"Are you all right? What's going on?" he asked, his voice harsh as if he feared some vile deed had been done.

Simon told him the bare facts, and Mr. Aldrich offered to escort them to the jailhouse. He assisted the ladies into his buggy, then walked beside Simon with his hand on his mare's bridle as they hurried to find the sheriff.

Charlie Wilson appeared in the open doorway of the jail before his visitors could reach it. He stepped outdoors, buckling his gun belt around his waist, and within a minute had been brought up-to-date on the news of the bungled efforts of Kenny Summers, his ploy to attack Ethel, and perhaps even get into the house to where Grace sat in the kitchen.

"I'll find the men Judge Hale recommended to me yesterday. I'm going to get a man in place to guard your house twenty-four hours a day. He mentioned three or four who would be reliable deputies and I'm going to provide all of them with a badge and we'll set out, leaving one at your house. First off, don't let anyone into your garden, Simon, for if there are tracks there or any trace of where the man might have gone, we don't want stray footprints to damage the evidence."

And then Charlie spoke quietly, words that Simon understood, vague as they might seem to an outsider. "Are you carrying it, Simon? Don't be fearful of using it."

Simon nodded and waved the banker on to his destination before he walked with the two women back to his house. "We should have set a guard for the daylight hours before now, I fear," he said, entering the gate and looking to where the man sent by the sheriff had watched the house till dawn. The grass was flattened by his presence, and an empty bottle, once filled with sarsaparilla, was the only remnant of his hours of nighttime duty.

Ethel walked over to pick it up, clucking her tongue in disapproval as she gripped it loosely, preparatory to tossing it in the rubbish bin. "A good thing it wasn't booze, or he'd have slept the night away," she said with a sniff of disapproval.

"No matter, Ethel, at least he was there and we slept knowing there was someone alert and caring for our well-being," Grace said, smiling at the frown Ethel wore, even as she muttered under her breath about men leaving messes behind, expecting someone to clean up after them.

Simon glanced at Grace, meeting her gaze, and they smiled, a moment of unity that pleased him. They went into the house and Ethel offered to make a pot of coffee for him, an offer Simon was pleased to accept, for it meant a few minutes with Grace at the table, perhaps an opportunity to mend some fences.

They spoke but little, but their eyes met and lingered, as if each rued the memory of the night past, and Simon thought the coffee he drank was the best he'd ever consumed. Grace drank a fresh cup of tea, and when Ethel went out into the yard, remembered to call after her to stay away from the back of the garden, as the sheriff had instructed them.

With a wave of her hand, Ethel went only as far as the green-bean patch, bending to fill her apron with enough of the fresh vegetables to prepare for dinner. She made her way to the tomato plants she had plundered with careless feet and propped several back up on the cages she had built for them from narrow pieces of wood lath. When all was in order she returned to the house, then sat upon the back porch with her lap full of beans.

"Grace, would you bring me a pan for these," she called out, and Grace was quick to oblige, handing a metal dish out the door before she returned to where Simon sat.

"Can we speak for a moment, Grace?" His words were quiet, almost a whisper, and she nodded, leading the way toward the parlor. But he would not follow her there, but took her hand and changed course, making the bedroom his destination. She glanced back at the kitchen and he only tugged at her, enclosing them in their bedroom without delay.

Chapter Twelve

"I can't tell you I've changed my mind, Grace. For I haven't. I still want you to stay inside the house, unless something happens as did the events that took place an hour ago. I won't apologize for making you angry with me or set you free of restraint. But I would have you know that I wish things were between us as they were before yesterday."

She stood before him, remembering the regret she'd felt as she dressed earlier, her thoughts as she realized he had risen without her knowledge, had left her to sleep with the window locked, the room quiet without his presence.

"I don't know what to say to you, Simon. My first urge was to run to you for safety when I saw Kenny out back. You've made me dependent upon you, and sometimes I feel that I'm less of a woman because of it."

He made a movement to halt her words and she put her hand against his mouth, closing his lips effectively. She thought she felt the pressure of that mouth move against her fingers and she almost smiled. Simon was Simon, no matter the circumstances, for he seemed unable to resist the touch of her flesh against his.

"Listen for just a moment. Hear me out. I would no doubt feel the same way should I be in your place, for I would protect you with my life, should it come to that. But there needs to be a partnership here, a coming together that will be pleasing to both of us."

He grinned and she realized she'd put her foot in her mouth. "I know what would please me. My thoughts on the matter are available should you want to hear them," he said, and she could only blush, for his intentions were obvious to her.

His penetrating gaze had made her blush. His hands lifted to fit themselves around her waist and he stepped closer to her, until their clothing provided but fragile layers of fabric between them. She knew the pressure of his wide chest against her breasts, the rise and lift of his arousal against her belly and the muscular strength of his thighs as he pressed her close. One hand rested in the small of her back, the better to bring her in line with his tall, masculine frame, and she felt a rush of feminine power as she recognized her effect on him.

He would, should she offer it, be more than willing to undress her, here and now, would lift and carry her to the bed, and would join her there, their bodies naked in the sunshine that made a mockery of the anger that had been so alive in the bed just hours ago.

She looked up into the dark gaze of a man who awaited her choice, who would walk away even now should she step back from him. And she could not do it. Could not deny his unspoken plea for her body.

And so she wrapped her arms around his neck, clung to him as might a child to her mother, seeking out his warmth, asking without words for his forbearance and offering herself with every scrap of humility she could summon.

"I was wrong, Simon, to withhold my body from you last night. For though I offered, it was not from my heart, and my arrogance overwhelms me when I remember the hurt in your eyes. I can only ask you to forgive me and help me to get past this time."

"There's nothing to forgive, Grace, for we were both at fault. I was harsh, demanding, and you were rightfully angry with me. I could not take one single embrace from you, without it being given freely, for it would be a mockery of the vows we made on our wedding day."

He stopped, his voice stilled, and she stepped back from him, recognizing the sudden flash of disappointment in his expression as she broke contact with his body. And then her fingers moved to the buttons she'd for the first time put in place such a short time ago. The dress fell from her to circle around her feet on the floor, and fast behind it flew her undergarments. She was already without covering on her feet. It was a simple enough matter for Simon to lift her and place her on the sheets that were still crumpled on the bed.

He watched her, his gaze filled with the beauty of creamy skin, a slim waist that he could almost circle with his hands and an expression on her face that invited his look and touch. His Grace was fast becoming more than a temptation to him. She'd become more than a desire he could take in his arms and then put aside when satisfied. For the passion that rose in his chest seemed to almost choke him. Certainly it did not allow him to speak, for he felt a fullness in his throat that guaranteed his voice would break should he allow it to invade the silence between them.

His clothing was removed in record time, his body seeking hers with a desperation he could barely contain and his kisses bathed her in warmth that knew no beginning and no end. Together they were utterly and unconditionally as one, for no matter that the future might hold harsh words and times of distress to come between them, for now, they existed as one being, one heart and one mind.

Early the next morning a group of men swarmed over the acreage behind the parsonage, for the vacant land behind the garden continued on to the river, a vast area, partly wooded where a man might easily be hidden amidst the treed area. Charlie led the hunt, intent on the footprints that had been left on the far side of the garden fence.

A man's boots had made deep impressions in the soil where the berry patch grew. The metal bowl that had been a missile against Kenny's flesh lay abandoned on the ground, the spill of red berries surrounding it seeming almost obscene. It was a desecration of the garden where the women had worked and felt safe.

But no longer, thought Grace as she watched the proceedings behind the house. For Grace and Ethel had lost the complacency they'd once enjoyed, able to come and go as they pleased. Now they cast fearful eyes on each man who came in view, until convinced of their purpose for being there, near the parsonage.

The group had been scouring the garden and the dirt beyond the fence for over an hour, several of them tracking into the woods and then returning to where Charlie led the search. He came to the house finally, meeting Grace at the back door, and she invited him into the kitchen.

There she offered him water and Ethel took a full bucket and a tin cup out to the men who still sought some clue as to Kenny Summers's direction once he'd left the garden.

"There's a lot of prints as far as the woods out back, some leading to the river, but it's hard to tell much, for a lot of men go fishing there, not to mention several of the neighborhood boys. They've even built a tree house, way up in a tall—"

Charlie's words halted abruptly and he rose from his seat at the table, heading for the back door as if the hounds of hell were behind him. "Jake Green, come on up here."

From the rear of the garden, a man made his way to Charlie's side, and the two men spoke together for mere minutes, their attention seemingly caught by something far beyond the garden fence.

"I'll check it out, Charlie." With a flurry of movement, Jake Green got the attention of two other men and they ran almost full tilt to the area of woods where the men had searched fruitlessly. With a shout of discovery, one of them waved at Charlie Wilson, and he jammed his hat down on his head and cleared the back fence in one leap, followed by two others who'd been sworn in as deputies. They disappeared just beyond the edge of the woods and in less than half an hour returned to the back of the house, Charlie doffing his hat as Grace and Ethel met him in the yard.

"He's been out there, apparently hiding in the tree house and in the bushes some. Those young fellas have put steps up in a tree and a platform up high. Should have checked it out right away, but none of the men thought of it. I sent Hank up and he found signs of someone being there, bits and pieces of food and a torn shirt."

"A dark plaid shirt?" Ethel asked and at Charlie's quick nod and another man's agreement, she explained further. "The man who came after me, and I'm sure it was Kenny Summers, was wearing a dark plaid shirt and I noticed he caught it on the fence and tore it. Happened to turn back for just a moment and almost forgot about it till now."

"There's no doubt about it, the man was Summers. I got a good look at him," Grace said firmly.

"It's a valuable piece of evidence. Now, if you'll excuse me, I'm going to get back to the investigation," Charlie said, flagging down a deputy as he headed back out the door.

"You and Shorty stay here with these two ladies till either me or the preacher comes back."

It took less than ten minutes for Simon to return, Belle close behind him. "Belle said she wants to talk to you, Grace. I knew there was no putting her off, so I brought her along with me."

Belle came into the hallway and sat down on a chair next to the clothestree. "I thought of something, Mrs. Grafton, and I wanted to talk to you about it."

"Talk away, then, Belle. And please call me Grace. Let's go into the kitchen and we'll make a pot of tea."

Grace cast a look at Simon which sent him out the front door and apparently allowed Belle to feel she could freely speak her mind to Grace. She hesitated but for a moment and her voice was hushed as she looked at Grace, seeming to notice all the younger woman's attributes.

"I remembered something that happened when that idiot was in my room, Grace. He got really mad, started yelling at me. Something about my hair being the wrong color. He accused me of changing the color to confuse him. I thought he seemed about half out of his mind, the way he was goin' on. He didn't like the color of my eyes, either, said they ought to be blue, not brown. And the good Lord knows I can't help the color of my eyes.

"I'll admit I lighten my hair with lemon juice. Have for years. If you sit in the sun, it makes your hair get lighter with the lemon on it. Men seem to go more for yellow hair for some reason and it was kind of dishwater blond when I was growing up.

"But I'll be doggoned if I could make head or tail out of the man's ramblings. He acted almost like he was crazy, saying he'd change my eyes back to blue. And that was before he started punching me. Before he bit me."

As though the pain were new, she flinched and bent her head. "I didn't think about it again till after you came to see me and then I remembered that your eyes were a pretty blue, something a man would notice, and your hair is real dark. It made me shiver to remember. It was like he wanted me to look different, maybe like you."

Grace placed the teapot on the table as she felt nausea grip her. Her legs seemed to be unable to hold her up. Without speaking she slid down the wall to sit on the floor. Belle scooted over, off the chair, and joined her, kneeling beside her and reaching for her hand.

"Sounds kinda silly, I guess, Grace. But I felt like we, you and me, was in this together. Like he's after both of us, maybe gets us mixed up in his head. I swear, the man's insane."

Simon appeared in the kitchen doorway, and Grace suspected he had listened to Belle's rambling narrative, for he pulled another chair from beside the table and joined them.

"I don't think you're far off, Belle. He's had a…a

fixation, I guess you'd call it, for Grace, ever since she lived at her uncle Joe's place. And now, since he can't have her, couldn't even find out where she was for a while there, he's been looking for her all over."

Belle pointed a finger at Simon. "Well, he found out she was living in your house, and he surely knows you've married her. I'll bet that really got under his skin if he was wanting her for himself. Makes you wonder how safe she is now."

Grace felt a sense of danger nearby, a dreadful feeling of evil looking on.

"What is it, sweetheart?" Simon asked, lifting her face, the better to see the expression she wore.

"Do you think he'll hurt people who know me? Maybe the Blackwoods or even my uncle? Uncle Joe is a good shot and well able to cope, but what about the people who were so good to me that first day when you and I went there to visit? They come to church every Sunday and always have a nice word for us. Do you think they're in danger and need protection? After all, they're two old people living out in the country alone, and—"

"I doubt there's much danger to them," Simon said quietly. "I'd say that Kenny's attentions are focused on you, and perhaps me."

Grace smiled sheepishly. "I'm just a worrier, I suspect. But maybe Charlie could have a deputy ride out there and check on them every day, so long as he has extra men right now."

Simon's mouth twisted into what was almost a smile. "I'll check with him, sweetheart. Just understand, I don't want you fretting about anyone else right now. Just keep yourself safe and I'll have less to worry about."

"I know that, Simon. You need to understand me, too. I can't bear for anything to happen to Ellie or Harold Blackwood, just because they've been nice to us."

Belle rose from her chair and turned her attention to Simon. "I didn't mean to cause a problem by coming here, Preacher. I probably should have kept things to myself, but I really felt like your wife should know."

"I understand, Belle. It's just that Grace has a unique bent to her. She can't help fussing and fretting about those she cares for. And Harold and Ellie fit into that group. I'm not being anything but careful with her."

"And with good reason," Belle said firmly, shooting a warning glance at Grace.

Simon asking the sheriff for a favor turned out to be easy, for when he showed up at the parsonage during his rounds that evening, Simon put the idea before him.

"I don't see why we can't make it a regular thing, sending someone out for a few hours, often enough so that anyone keeping an eye on the place wouldn't know when the next deputy might turn up. I'll start in the morning. I think Grace is all right with just one man here with her."

"I'll be at the church for the morning hours, so she only needs a man close by till about noon," Simon told him. And with that, the arrangements were put in place.

In the last moments before Grace went to bed, Simon took a turn about the property lines, walking past the garden, then around the front of the house. The deputy on duty there lifted a hand and greeted him.

"You've got a lonesome job," Simon told him.

"Beats draggin' drunks out of the saloon," said Jake Green. "Although I haven't gotten that detail yet. I'm just an extra hand while Charlie's huntin' down our man. Sure hope we get some results soon. My wife's getting tired of being alone so much. But then she said it was worth my time and more if we could keep just one girl safe in town."

"My thoughts, exactly," Simon returned, turning to walk toward the front porch. "My thanks, Jake." And with that wave, he entered the house.

"Things look calm and peaceful out there," he told Grace. He opened the curtains when they'd finished undressing, to let the fresh air blow through the room. "I don't feel real easy with that window open, but Jake will keep a good eye out for us."

The breeze blew nicely, making it more comfortable to sleep in the August heat, and Grace was again thankful for the good folks of the town, all of them willing to help.

Morning brought but one deputy to relieve Jake Green and he took up his post near the back porch. Ethel took out a cup of coffee and fresh cinnamon rolls to him, making his duty less tedious, and he was properly grateful.

With two women working together, the house was neat and tidy and Ethel cleared the table after they ate. Grace washed up the dishes and offered a few suggestions as Ethel made up a grocery list.

"We don't need a lot, but if I'm going to bake a cake for dessert tonight, I'll need another pound or two of butter. And the vanilla bottle is almost empty," Ethel muttered as she scribbled down the items on her list. "I won't be long, Grace. And Shorty is out back to keep an eye on things," Ethel said as she scooped up her basket from the pantry and headed for the door.

So Grace was alone with the stalwart company of Shorty, who sat beneath a willow tree near the garden. She suspected he was snoozing, but didn't have the heart to wake him, since he'd be stuck out there until almost dark, awaiting his relief.

She'd barely turned from the back door when a

shout from beyond the riverbank spun her around. A young boy was waving frantically and shouting for help, awakening Shorty in moments.

Without hesitation, Shorty jumped the back fence and met the boy halfway, bending his head to listen to the disjointed words he spoke. With a wave at Grace and a shout warning her to stay in the house, he ran into the woods. The boy came toward the house then, and Grace opened the back door.

"What's happened?" she asked, fearful for Shorty's safety.

"That man told me to get the sheriff, ma'am. A big man's got my sister and she's hollerin' something awful. Somebody's gotta help Josie, missus," the boy cried, tears flowing down his face, his whole body trembling with obvious fear for his sister's plight.

"You run across the road and down toward town to the sheriff's office, sonny. Tell him to come right away. And stop by the church and let the preacher know that there's trouble here. I'll see what I can do to help." Without forethought, only knowing that a small child was in danger, Grace ran to the back fence, scrambled over and headed through the patch of woods to where the river flowed past the edge of town. Surely Shorty could not be far ahead of her.

Calling out his name, she ran on, almost tripping

over an exposed tree root in her haste. With the last breath she could drag forth from her lungs, she called out the child's name. "Josie, where are you?"

Her feet fairly flew as she made her way through the trees, not a long route by any means, but sufficient cover to hide the riverbank from her view until she came upon Shorty, lying across the path. She bent to him, her hand touching his chest. He was breathing, but unconscious, and she found the source of his problem readily when a knot on the side of his head met her searching fingers.

"Josie." She muttered the name beneath her breath and stood, looking around her for the little girl. And then she called her again. "Josie. Josie, where are you?"

The sound of a child crying reached her ears and she hastened down the path, looking in vain for the little girl. And then felt a muscular arm wind its way around her neck. Another arm clutched at her waist.

And a rough voice spoke her name.

"Where is she? Where is Grace?" Ethel was breathless, having run the last hundred feet or so once she saw the young boy waving from the front porch of the parsonage.

The child let out a cry of distress. "My sister Josie is down by the river. A man grabbed her and when I hollered, a fella ran to find her and then the lady came to help."

Ethel's hand covered her chest, as if her heart had failed her. "Oh, my… Where's Simon?" Her basket hit the ground as she raced for the church, and the door to Simon's study flew open as she reached it.

"What's wrong, Ethel? Where's—"

His worst fears were realized as he caught sight of Ethel's face and heard the small boy's continuing pleas for help. Without pause, the boy hot on his heels, Simon jumped the back fence, his long legs carrying him down the riverbank and into the woods. Ahead of him he could make out another child's voice, and a small girl ran toward him.

"Jasper, Jasper, where are you?"

"That's my Josie," the boy said breathlessly from behind Simon. "That's my sister."

The girl tore heedlessly through the trees and ran into Simon's arms, seeking refuge. He held her against his shoulder and comforted her. "You're all right, Josie. Where is the man? Which way did he go?"

Josie cried and sobbed, her fright sending her almost into hysterics. "That bad man hit a fella and he fell down in the woods." The child reached for him again, hanging on his shirt sleeve.

"Mister, you better listen to me. The man had a horse and he took the pretty lady with him,"

Josie shouted, and the last of her words were aimed at Simon's back as he plowed his way toward the swiftly flowing water.

"Grace." His whisper was audible only to himself, but the despair was reflected in his eyes as he turned back to look at Ethel. She held the child in her arms, and he waved her off, not wanting her to bring the child closer. For inside the wooded area lay Shorty's still-unconscious form in the middle of the path. A path made by the feet of many of the neighborhood children who sought out the shady dell for their games.

"Get Charlie Wilson," Simon shouted over his shoulder at Ethel, by now a hundred feet behind him. He shoved his gun into his waistband, heading back to the river. There might be no sense in going there, but if there were tracks he'd find them. And follow.

"Go wake up Jake Green and find all the available men in town. We'll start down by the river behind the parsonage." Charlie's orders were succinct and easily followed, for the man who'd been so directed turned and ran the length of town, putting his head in at each doorway beginning with the general store. Then the bank, the hardware store, the shoe repair, the newspaper office and, lastly, the barbershop. In each doorway, he shouted out a simple message.

"The preacher's wife is gone. Some fella stole her up from behind the parsonage."

And behind him, the men of the town left what they were doing and followed, gathering up mounts from the livery stable and along the road wherever there was a hitching rail with horses awaiting their owners. Whether the mounts they took were their own or another man's, it made no difference, only that they all be mounted and ready to search.

Mr. Aldrich ran with the barber's apron still firmly attached to his neck, half-shaven, but ready for battle. At the livery stable, Charlie snatched the bridle for an extra mount, knowing that Simon would not be left behind and, not willing to give up his own horse, decided it would be wise to take an extra one along for Simon's use.

Ethel's garden suffered a major calamity as the men rode through the yard and over the fence, through the trees and down to the riverbank. Simon could be seen, running along the bank to the west, obviously following tracks, and the men caught up with him quickly.

Charlie slowed the pace of his gelding and held out the reins of the mare he'd brought with Simon in mind. Without pause, Simon was on the horse's back, riding without a saddle, waving the men to follow him.

"I sent Shorty out to the Cumberland place. He was still staggering a bit, but he knows what needs to be done. Figured Joe could send his men to help look for them," Charlie said, holding his mount to a trot, lest he miss the tracks of the horse they followed. And then the tracks went into the river and they were left without a clue. If Summers had continued on to the west, they'd find hoofprints farther along. But if he'd gone into the woods across the river, they'd have no way of knowing it.

Charlie sent two men on horseback to ford the water with instructions to shoot three times if they found any trail to follow. Simon was ahead of him, riding in the shallows, watching for any disturbance along the side of the water, where the man might have turned to ride cross-country.

"Nothing yet?" Charlie asked, reining in alongside Simon.

Simon only shook his head, unable to think clearly. "We have to find her, Charlie. I fear he'll take out all his meanness on her. Hell, the man could kill her in a heartbeat. She's so little, so defenseless."

"We've got over twenty men mounted and searching, son. We'll find them. Just keep watching for tracks."

On the other side of the river, three shots rang out and Charlie pulled his horse up short. "Across the river, all but two of you. You, Jake and Tom, stay on this side and watch for tracks. He may cut back across."

The water was thankfully not deep and the horses forded at a narrow point where the shallows gave them good footing. Reaching the opposite bank, they set off, north into the woods and a bit east in order to find the two men who had fired the signal.

Joe Cumberland had eight men in their saddles in mere minutes when the news came with Shorty's arrival at the ranch. "We'll ride toward the river and keep an eye out on both sides of the road. He may cut across anywhere, so we'd better split up into pairs," Joe shouted hastily. Taking Shorty with him, he spurred his horse to a gallop and they covered the flat ground rapidly.

"Grace and the sheriff think Kenny might have a beef with the Blackwoods. You think he'd go there?"

"It wouldn't hurt to check. Let's go," Joe said.

Fearful of obliterating the tracks, should any be visible, Charlie and Simon rode with caution, watching the riverbank and keeping a close eye on the men who patrolled the opposite side of the water.

"There. Look there, Charlie." Simon pointed at a roughened patch ahead, where tracks led into the river again, the horse having slid down the embankment, leaving a clear trail behind.

"We're not too far behind them," Charlie

said. "Keep it quiet. If he's anywhere close, he'll hear us."

Thankful for the sandy ground they traveled, they rode as rapidly as possible, but kept strict silence. Men's voices traveled in the air and the woods were well covered by searchers, but Simon felt a clutch of fear as he considered where Summers might have taken Grace.

The river went under a bridge just ahead and the road above was the one leading to the Blackwood Farm. The two men exchanged looks of intent, and without a word, their mounts were guided up the bank and onto the well-worn road. Fortunately it made its way beneath a veritable arbor of trees, making it cooler than had been the case in the bright sunshine.

The horses were fresh and willing and they traveled at top speed, silent but for the heavy breathing of the men, who feared the worst and felt incapable of bringing a halt to it.

Ahead of them, perhaps a hundred yards or so, two horses galloped in tandem, one of the figures that of Joe Cumberland.

"Didn't take him long, did it?" Charlie breathed harshly.

Simon was more than thankful for the man who rode beside him and even more so that they had two more men on the same track. For he was certain that they were on the right trail, that even though there were no fresh hoofprints to follow, their prey had come in this direction.

"Hold up, Charlie. Look here." Joe pointed to the hayfield beside the road, where the hay appeared to have been flattened by the passage of a horse. The hay bent low and offered a silent clue as to the rider who had so recently covered this same ground.

A horse, heavily burdened by the looks of it, was heading across the pastureland ahead, its route on a beeline for Harold Blackwood's place. "Charlie." He shouted the man's name and then bent low over his mare's neck and urged the horse on.

Behind him, he heard Charlie's voice and knew he'd seen him changing course. The figure ahead of him disappeared from sight then, over a hilly area and through a stand of trees.

Behind him Charlie fell back a bit, but ahead of him he saw Joe off to the right, heading from the town road across the pasture. For the first time in the past hour, he felt a shard of hope drive out the despair that had him so firmly in its grip.

She was here, not far ahead. He could feel it. He knew it.

His horse came over the hill and there was no sign of the rider ahead, only the familiar shape of Harold Blackwood's barn.

Grace kicked and shrieked, all to no avail. The man who clutched at her with a painful grip did not shift his hold for a moment, only held her firmly over the saddle before him. The horn pressed into her belly and she felt tears of pain she could not control as each step the horse took brought her down afresh in unforgiving punishment.

And then he pulled her back against his body and she felt the unmistakable bulge at his crotch that announced his state of arousal. Her face was pressed against his leg, her cheek shoved past his knee, and she closed her eyes, for the dirt had almost blinded her, flying from the horse's front hooves past her in a veritable windstorm of dust and pebbles. Her face stung from the tiny blows like buckshot from a gun and she felt the shade of a tree pass over the horse, then another animal nearby nickered a greeting.

There was no way of knowing where he'd taken her, but she knew that the man who held her down with cruel hands was Kenny Summers. She'd caught sight of him with a small girl in his grip and, fearful of the child's welfare, had run heedlessly to help her, only to be grabbed by Kenny and thrown over the back of his horse.

At least Grace had gained the little girl's freedom. Now as they continued riding, she struggled and felt his fist cuff her cheek, heard him swear and felt his grip on her tighten, as though he realized that should she fall he dare not go back for her. "Your stupid preacher man is sure to be close behind what with all the squawkin' and squallin' that young'un was doing back there," he grated.

Grace lifted her arm to cover her eyes and Kenny twisted it behind her. "Lay still, bitch." His words were a snarl, his body unwashed and smelling of sweat and manure. If there was a way to escape this brute, she'd find it. Somehow she had to get away, for Simon would blame himself should she be killed in such a fashion. And yet, she'd felt compelled to help the child in peril.

The horse slowed again. She heard his hooves clatter against a harder surface and then he slid to a stop, the surroundings darker, the sunshine somehow obscured. "They won't be lookin' for us here," Kenny panted, hauling her from his saddle and down to the floor.

Grace smelled hay and the ripe scent of manure. They were in a barn, and there appeared to be no one else in the building. Kenny's horse backed up into the corral, and strong arms lifted her, dragging her into a stall where straw covered the floor beneath her.

His breathing was harsh and heavy, his breath fetid in her face, and she turned her face to the side, closing her eyes, unwilling to let him know she was awake, her mind racing to feel some small lessening of pressure in his grip upon her.

He lay upon her and she lost her breath, his body a solid weight against her chest and belly.

All was silent but for his muttered words, threats and promises that chilled her blood within her. "Thought you'd fooled me, didn't you? Guess you know who's the one in charge now, don't ya?"

Harsh, cruel hands gripped the front of her dress and tore it in shreds, to well below her waist. Again he gripped fabric and she felt the sheer material of her chemise split beneath his strength. Her eyes opened then as she looked up into his face and she shuddered as saliva dripped from his open mouth onto her flesh, his teeth meeting in a savage grin as he looked down at her naked breasts.

"Thought I'd never get to try a taste of this, Gracie, didn't you?" His head lowered to her throat and she stiffened beneath him. "Come on, girlie. You know you like it. Let me have what you been givin' that preacher man."

Her head twisted and turned; she was barely able to force breath from her lungs and then she felt his teeth against the skin of her breast. Knew the degradation of filthy hands touching her flesh, a mouth fit for a pig's trough against her throat and then again on her breast.

With her last breath, drawn from lungs squeezed almost beyond pain, her voice rose in a strangled sob. She screamed as his teeth bit down and she felt the blessed blackness descend.

Chapter Thirteen

Joe Cumberland leaped from his horse before the animal stopped moving, then released the reins, letting his mount free. Flattening himself against the side of the barn, he peered around the corner, fearful of a bullet being aimed in his direction, but knowing that his niece was in mortal danger. Because of his own stupidity.

And for that he might never forgive himself. Hoofbeats resounded across the meadow, heading toward the barn, and Joe lifted a hand in warning, for he'd seen, there in the corral, the empty saddle of the horse Kenny Summers was fond of riding. The animal was covered with foam, and his body heaved as he fought to breathe.

And then, splitting the silence, a woman's voice screamed aloud. A cry ridden with such pain, such despair, he could only shudder at the sound. Behind him, Simon Grafton left his mount with a single movement and Joe stepped before him, lest he burst into the barn unarmed.

Standing in the open doorway, his rifle ready, Joe was stunned by the sight of Kenny, standing within the shadows of a stall. Kenny's hands worked at his suspenders, sliding them over his shoulders, allowing his trousers to fall to his knees.

Behind him, Simon's utterance was a growl of fury, and Joe lifted his gun, aiming high, lest he hit the woman on the floor, her clothing torn into shreds. His shot struck its target and Kenny Summers flew the length of the stall, his head hitting resoundingly against the manger.

"Grace." With but a single sound, Simon pushed past Joe, shoving him aside and dropping to his knees beside the still form of his wife. He bent his head, his dark hair almost covering her nakedness, his face at her throat. From the layers of fabric that lay split asunder, a steady stream of blood flowed to stain the ground beneath her.

Simon tore his shirt off, uncaring about buttons or seams, and covered Grace with it, lifting her from the straw and holding her against his chest. His eyes were anguished as he caught sight of Joe behind him, and for a moment Joe was silent, fearful of the blood that flowed, knowing that its source was the girl in Simon's arms.

Simon lifted her, turned with her toward her uncle, and tears ran down his cheeks, his bereft cry rising to the rafters. And down his trousers, dripping from Grace's still form was a flow of blood, forming an obscene picture to the man who watched.

In the corral two other horsemen had dismounted and stood at the doorway, their faces dismayed, their expressions uncertain. Charlie and Shorty watched in silence as Simon appealed to Joe.

"Is she breathing? Feel her face, Joe. I can't feel any breath from her mouth."

Joe stepped forward and bent his head to Grace's face, his cheek beneath her nose.

"She's breathing, son. She's breathing. Just go easy now. Take her to the house."

"Where's the blood coming from?" Shorty asked, his face drawn, his lungs gasping, as if seeing the young woman had taken his wind from him.

"Was she shot? I heard a gun fire."

"No, she's not been shot," Simon said, turning and carrying her from the barn, his steps slow as he made his way to the house where Harold Blackwood stood in the doorway.

"What's happened? Is that Grace?" He held the door open and Simon walked into the kitchen, to where Harold's wife, Ellie, had been cooking at the stove.

"She's bleeding," Ellie said. "Get towels, Harold.

Right quick. And you, Simon, take her in the bedroom. Put her on the bed."

But Simon could not release her from his hold and instead sat on the edge of the wide bed, holding Grace in his arms. He balanced her across his knees and with his free hand lifted his shirt from her breast. Marks marred the soft flesh and he bent a bit to see better where the blood flow originated. His hand was tender, his touch gentle as he lifted the soft weight of her right breast and exposed the tender underside.

Behind him, Ellie gasped and began to cry. "That bastard bit her. Look at the teeth marks."

Simon nodded. "Give me a clean cloth and warm water, Ellie. I'll bathe it." He held the cloth against her torn flesh and his tears fell against his own hand as he gently wiped the bloodstains from her skin.

"A pad or a towel—something to soak it up, Ellie." He waited, holding out his hand, and Ellie took the clean washcloth from next to the basin and folded it in fourths, placing it in his palm. He laid it carefully against the still-bleeding wound and held it in place.

"Simon." It was Charlie in the doorway and he came closer. Simon pulled the damp cloth over Grace's breast and lifted his head, his gaze meeting that of the sheriff.

"She's alive, Simon. And he didn't—"

"I know." The reply was bitten out, his voice harsh and grating. Had Charlie not known, he would not have recognized it as coming from Simon Grafton, for he sounded like a man whose rage had not known release.

"I wish I'd killed him, Charlie. I should have been the one to avenge my wife. I failed her all the way around, and then at the final moment, when I should have been the one to shoot, I let Joe handle it. Not consciously, but my only thought was to get to Grace. I feared he'd killed her for a moment, and then I thought it would be justice if a man could die more than once."

He rocked Grace in his arms, sitting there on the side of the bed, and when she moved, her body spasming against him, she cried out. He winced, his eyes closing, his teeth biting into his bottom lip, as if he could not bear to hear her pain uttered aloud.

"Simon." It was but a whisper but he bent to her, his lips against her brow, then her cheek. Her eyes opened a bit and she spoke his name again, a painful sound that caused the sheriff and Joe to look aside lest they allow their own tears to fall.

For Simon there was no such shelter, for the salty drops that fell from his eyes blended with hers and slid silently against her cheeks.

"I'm here, Grace. I have you, sweetheart. No one will hurt you again."

"But *he* did, Simon. It hurts so bad…" Her words faded and her breath caught as if she could not speak aloud.

"Oh, baby…" His tears flowed unceasingly and his arms held her tenderly, careful not to touch the damaged breast. And when his next words came they were dark and filled with a hatred no man could have doubted as he looked directly at Charlie. "Is he dead?"

"I shot him," Joe said tightly. "A head shot, Simon. He hasn't moved and he won't, ever again. Not till we pick him up and dump him six feet under."

His wide shoulders shuddered and Simon lifted his head. "Ellie, some more water please, and another clean pad."

The men in the room looked aside as Ellie moved to stand in front of Simon, moving the cloth that hid Grace's breast. They heard her gasp, then the silence as Ellie did as Simon directed, wiping the blood flow, her soft words telling them that it had slowed considerably, and a tight bandage should solve the issue.

Simon held Grace almost erect in his lap, her face against his throat, while Ellie wrapped a long piece of fabric torn from a sheet around her middle, holding the thick pad in place, bringing the bleeding to a slow seepage that looked to be slowing even as Simon watched.

She tenderly draped Simon's shirt over Grace's breasts, then searched through the closet for one of Harold's for Simon to wear. With Charlie's help, he slid first one arm, then the other into it. "Thanks, Ellie."

She only patted his shoulder and helped him to rise from the bed. "I think you need to take her home," she said quietly. "Let the doctor come to your place, Simon, and check her out."

He stood before his friends and they gathered around him, Joe's hand on Grace's head. "Horses," Charlie said, heading for the door, motioning Shorty to go with him as they went through to the kitchen and out the back door. Behind the barn, the horses waited, their reins touching the ground, Simon's still without a saddle.

"He'd better ride mine," Charlie said. "I'll take the mare. He'll need the saddle to balance with." Shorty nodded and together they rode up to the back of the house, waiting as Joe held the door open for Simon to bear his wife from the house.

"I'm heavy," she murmured against his throat, and he only shook his head carefully.

"Take her, Joe, till I get on the horse," he said, his voice having lost its roughness, control returning with an effort. Joe lifted his niece into his arms and held her with gentle care, then with Charlie's aid, they lifted her into Simon's arms. He held her as though she were made of priceless porcelain and bent once more to touch his lips to her brow as he turned his mount toward home.

Once they arrived back at the parsonage, the doctor appeared within minutes after Simon carried his bundle into the bedroom, for Shorty had ridden ahead to alert him that he was needed. Simon had placed Grace on the waiting bed, Ethel having pulled back the sheet and quilt in preparation when Shorty rode ahead to let her know the small caravan was on its way.

When the doctor entered the bedroom, it was to find Simon on his knees beside the bed, one arm holding Grace still, lest she move and cause herself more pain. His other arm had found its place beneath her head and she had turned to lay her cheek close to his shoulder. He looked up and met the doctor's eyes, both men wearing the same look of grief.

The doctor spoke first. "I reckon I know what he did to her. He marked her as he did the woman over at the saloon, didn't he?" And at Simon's nod, the medical man shook his head and muttered a word he was seldom prone to use.

"There's not a lot we can do for it, but Belle knows of a salve that worked well for her. One of the ladies at the saloon made it out of some sort of leaves and cobwebs, mixed with a strange kind of tea. Don't ask me any more than that, Simon. I don't question stuff like that. I just know enough to use what I'm given and thank the good Lord that there's those in this world who know a different kind of medicine than I learned in college."

"Will you send Belle over?" Simon asked, for he would gladly seek help for Grace from whatever source was available. And the doctor seemed to believe in what Belle had to offer for Grace's healing.

The doctor spoke up. "She'll no doubt be here before I'm done looking at Grace. I sent Shorty to tell her she was needed."

"Thanks, Doc." Simon bowed his head and moved back a bit, giving the doctor room to work.

"Simon." Grace's voice was soft, but her hand lifted to him and the doctor merely nodded and waited.

"I'm here, sweetheart. Don't move, baby. We're gonna take the bandage off so the doctor can look at it."

"I don't want—"

"I won't touch you till Belle gets here, Mrs. Grafton. She's got some salve that works for this sort of injury. To prevent infection."

From the front of the house, Simon heard Belle's voice, then that of Ethel speaking. The ladies appeared in mere seconds at the bedroom door and Belle's eyes were reddened, her mouth firm, as if she withheld tears.

"Belle." He greeted her simply and she put her hand on his arm.

"Let me see her, Reverend."

He moved, only a bit, for Grace would not release his hand from her grasp, and he would not make her cry out by leaving her side.

But the woman knelt beside him and touched Grace's arm. "I'm here, Grace. It's Belle, come to see you…"

The blue eyes opened and Simon saw within her such pain, such darkness, it was all he could do not to look away, but he unflinchingly met her gaze as she turned her head toward him, his mouth lifting in a smile that cost him much. And then she looked at Belle and her nod was a greeting in itself.

Simon left her with Belle, alone but for the doctor standing by. It was out of man's hands, be he husband or doctor. Perhaps another woman, one who had known the same pain, the same cruel treatment from a man, was what Grace needed now.

And as for Simon, he knew not where his healing would be found. He walked to the church next door and entered the front door, walking down the aisle to where his pulpit stood to one side of the congregation. He knelt at the altar, looking up to the place where he stood on Sunday mornings and guilt fell upon him as had the stones on Stephen in the Bible.

He'd wanted to kill, and kill with violent means, for he knew he would have gladly pounded the brute into the ground, bloodied him and battered him beyond recognition. And such violence could not live in the heart and soul of a man who had vowed to serve the church and obey his Maker. He could only be thankful that he'd not been the one to pull the trigger. And yet, he felt he'd somehow failed Grace by letting another avenge her.

Grace. The woman who needed him now. The girl who lay on his bed, with an open wound perhaps still seeping blood, and her husband still aching for revenge. Revenge on a man already beyond such things. A man who would lie in a grave come tomorrow. A man who would suffer eternal death.

He was unworthy, both of the title he held that bound him to this church, and of the name of husband. For in both, he had failed. He knew, as surely as he drew his next breath, that the ache in his heart would not be healed until Grace was whole again. And he feared it would be a long row to hoe before they reached that time. For though her body would heal there was an even greater, deeper wound in her soul.

And he feared that in his own strength he might never find a remedy for it.

If the town thought it strange that Grace's most regular visitor was a woman from the saloon,

Simon cared but little. For the word had gone around, thanks to the ever-reliable grapevine, that Belle was in possession of a salve made originally by the Indian tribes who had once been in the area, and that salve was known to work miracles of healing. So Simon accepted Belle into his home with a smile of kindness, for the woman's only mission in life seemed to be the healing of the dark-haired female who lay within the walls of the parsonage.

As for Grace, she slept. More than Simon thought was good for her, more than the doctor himself thought was healthy, but according to Belle, they must leave her alone and allow her body to heal as it would. Grace awoke when Belle came to her, spoke quietly with the woman and hugged her when she left. And if Simon wondered at the bond that formed between them, he did not discuss it with anyone, for whatever made Grace feel better, whatever helped her convalescence, it would be done.

And when he undressed at night and lay down beside her, she turned to him, at first with hesitation. Indeed for the first night, she held herself apart, only touching his hand or arm, allowing him to kiss her, but unwilling to have his arms encircle her.

Simon grieved privately for the loss of intimacy, not that he yearned to make love with his bride, but that he dearly wanted to hold her in his arms. It seemed, though, that she could not allow it, and he took what he could get, which was precious little, to his way of thinking.

But he did not utter a word of complaint, only rose each morning and brought her tea to the bed, sitting with her while she drank it, watching as ounces and pounds of flesh dropped from her slender frame.

And in all of the days that passed, he dragged with him, dogging each step, the guilt of his hatred toward the man who had caused such harm to a helpless woman. He could not speak of it to Grace, for the syllables of Kenny's name were not allowed to touch her ears. He could only hold within himself the burden of his blackened soul, for even the bishop, when he'd called on Simon the week before, did his best to console the young man, prayed with him and tried to bring a sense of healing and forgiveness to Simon.

But in vain.

And then one day, when Grace refused the tea he offered, when she'd turned her face away, he reached a point of pain he could no longer bear. He left the bedroom and went to the kitchen. When he returned he was carrying a bowl of soup Ethel had prepared, knowing it was Grace's favorite. She lay before him on the bed with her eyes fixed on the ceiling.

"Sweetheart, I want you to eat some soup," he said softly, sitting beside her. "Let me help you to sit up. I'll hold the bowl for you, love."

Once more she moved her head in a negative gesture and he was crushed by her refusal, not because he felt it was directed at him, but because the food did not appeal to her.

"Grace, I need to talk to you," he said gently. He lifted her to lean against three pillows, stacking them against the headboard and carefully propping her there. She closed her eyes, as if she would thus escape him, and he bent to her, kissing her forehead.

She froze, her eyes flying open, and he took her hand in his. "I can't bear it if you won't let me touch you, Grace. Please try not to cringe from me."

Her eyes filled with bitter tears and they fell to her nightgown. "I'm so sorry, Simon. I truly am. I know I'm a great burden on you, and I don't know what to do about it."

"Stop, Grace. Stop right there. Don't you ever again call yourself a burden. You are the light that brightens my day. I have no sunshine without you, and my soul is dark with your pain. I can only pray for guidance, for you don't give me any hint as to what I can do to help you. You must eat or you will wither away to nothing. I fear for your very life, my heart. I can only coax you to take a bite."

He halted for he could speak no longer. His voice was hoarse, his words but a whisper, and his throat ached with unshed tears.

"I told you I'm nothing but a burden, Simon. You've been so good to me, and I can't even tell you I love you. And you know I do. You must." Her eyes beseeched him and her face was woebegone with the sorrow that she bore.

"Do you love me, Grace? You've never told me, you know. And now I need your love more than ever before. I need to know that you care for me, that I'm not a weight you must bear."

She looked up at him and for the first time since the night he'd brought her here to this bed, she smiled. Not a smile he would have recognized in the past, but a softening of her lips, a movement of the flesh in her cheek where a dimple had remained unseen for many days.

"Never think I don't love you, Simon. You are the only reason I awake in the mornings."

"Will you do something for me, sweetheart? Please, I beg you with all my heart."

"I'll try. You know that." And as if she were exhausted from the few words she'd spoken, she closed her eyes.

"Don't open your eyes, Grace. Just let me put a bit of soup in your mouth."

He waited for endless seconds, a minute or more, and when he'd come to understand that she cared little for nourishment, and it seemed his heart would burst with the pain of it, she opened her mouth. Just a little, enough for a spoon to pass between her lips and teeth.

"That's my baby," he said gently, lifting a scant spoonful of broth to her mouth, a spoonful she swallowed and then her lips closed again.

"Sweetheart, we'll wait for a minute and then try again. Will you do that for me?" He struggled with impatience, he fought against the urge to coax her further and his heart merely rejoiced that she had made the effort he'd asked of her.

And in a minute or so, she spoke again. "All right, Simon. I'll eat some more."

Her lips parted and with a slow, steady hand, he brought the bowl of the spoon to her lips again and watched as she moved her lips. He saw the effort she made when the mouthful lay against her tongue and then rejoiced when her throat moved and the few drops were swallowed.

"Ah, Grace. You make me so happy. I feel like laughing out loud, sweetheart. Will you let me know when you can try another swallow?"

She nodded, a barely perceptible movement of her head, but he was aware of each breath she took and such a nod did not escape his eye. He heard the rustle of a garment behind him and turned to look over his shoulder. In the doorway, Ethel stood, tears falling, but her lips were smiling, a look akin to happiness on her face.

He sat with Grace for an hour, and in all, she ate perhaps half a cup of the chicken broth.

"That'll do for now, sweetheart. I'll let you rest a bit. We'll try again before bedtime, shall we?"

She looked at him and he was blessed by the love that shone from blue eyes, his heart receiving the message she did not speak aloud. Her lips puckered just a bit, as if she would pout, and he knew. Knew without words that she would kiss him should he bend to her now.

"Grace?" He leaned toward her and her hand lifted to touch his cheek. "Grace, may I kiss you?"

Her lips moved and he bent closer, careful not to infringe, lest she not respond to him. But the hand that touched his cheek moved to the back of his head and she exerted just a bit of pressure there, guiding him where she would, until his mouth pressed gently against hers, until her breath flowed from her lips to his.

He prayed she would not open her eyes, for he could not halt the tears. For a man who had not shed one tear since he was but a lad, he'd broken some sort of record of late, he decided. And yet, he did not rue one drop that fell, for he'd been blessed beyond measure to have the response she'd offered him, freely and without pressure on his part.

And so when he undressed that night and crawled in to lie beside her, he dared to reach for her hand, and when she clasped his fingers with hers, he lifted and bent to her. "May I kiss you good-night?"

"Oh, yes, Simon. Please." It was almost Grace's voice again, he thought, weak perhaps, but with the same soft melody in each syllable she spoke.

He kissed her twice, gently but thoroughly. And then put his head on his pillow. She'd eaten again before he turned out the light and he whispered words of praise in her ear, lying beside her, feeling for the first time that all would be well.

In the morning, she was awake when he opened his eyes, and her face was but inches from his.

"Are you all right?" he asked, startled, for she never awoke before he'd left the bed to get dressed. And yet, perhaps she had. That thought bade him lie still and he touched her cheek, brushing a strand of dark hair from her face. "Will you try a bit of tea for me, sweetheart? I'll put milk and sugar in it for you."

She nodded, and then opened her mouth a bit, pushing the words out as if it were an effort to speak. "Yes, Simon. If you'll kiss me first. I've missed you."

It was an ongoing time of healing. From that day onward, she ate a bit more each time he brought food to her, graduating to scrambled eggs, then milk toast. The day she ate a spoonful of mashed potatoes, all creamed nicely with milk and butter, he rejoiced. And thought for the first time that they would finally make it. And again he sought to coax her.

"If I help you, will you put on your robe and sit in a chair for a while?"

Her nod was quick, and he snatched her robe from the wardrobe. Putting it over her shoulders, he guided her hands into the sleeves, then waited till she could catch her breath.

"Let me help you get up and I'll tie the belt for you." She clasped his hands in hers and he lifted her. "Will you sit on the rocker?"

She shook her head and took his hand, leaning heavily on his arm. They had gone perhaps three feet, when he scooped her from her feet and carried her. "Where shall we go, sweetheart?"

"The kitchen." She spoke the word clearly and when he left the bedroom with her, he saw Ethel's shadow pass the doorway in the back of the house.

"Ethel. Pull out a chair for us, please," he called, his smile wide as he carried his wife triumphantly down the stairway and through the hall.

"On my lap?" he asked softly, offering her the choice, and to his relief, she nodded.

"Next time, I'll sit alone," she said.

He held her against himself, her head tucked beneath his chin, his arms around her, holding her fast, lest she slide to the floor. Her weight was frightening, he'd decided when he'd lifted her, for she was thin, almost to the point of skin and bones, but he would not mention it, for fear of discouraging her.

"Is it time for breakfast?" she asked.

"Breakfast is whenever you want it, love," he told her. "Right now is fine, don't you think, Ethel?"

To which the stalwart housekeeper nodded briskly before she turned to cut a slender slice from a fresh loaf of bread. She buttered it, spread a thin layer of honey atop and then cut it into four pieces and placed it on a plate.

"My mother used to call these toast slices soldiers when I was small," Simon said, lifting one to his lips, biting off the crust, then offering her the soft, inner layer.

They ate the bread, Simon offering her small bites until the slice of bread was eaten. Ethel brought a cup of tea to her, prepared as she liked it, with milk and sugar added, and she sipped it carefully.

It was too much to hope that she would not tire rapidly, and he was not disappointed when she signaled her need to return to the bed. He carried her in, removed the robe and put her in the center of the bed. Then, as she watched with wide eyes, he took his trousers off and lay beside her, pulling up the sheet.

"I need you, Grace. Please let me lie with you."

She lifted her head and he understood her silent plea, for he slipped his arm beneath her neck and she settled into place, there where she was wont to sleep during the early days of their marriage. And in less time than he could have imagined, she was asleep, her mouth open just a bit, her eyes shut and her breathing regular.

He did not stir, even when Ethel came to the door. For he only lifted his hand and waved and heard the latch close behind her.

And when the doctor came to call the next day, it was to find his patient on the edge of the bed, robe in place, slippers on her feet and a half smile on her lips.

"Grace. My word, I can't believe the change in you. I declare, you have roses in your cheeks."

And even Simon could not deny that observation, for she had a glow about her that soothed his aching heart. He winked at her and his lips curved in a wide smile.

It was a gradual process, for every day did not bring as much progress as those first few. But in two weeks' time, she was rising for all her meals, making her way to the table on Simon's arm, and her bones had begun to be covered with a modest amount of flesh.

At least Simon didn't have to shake the sheets to find her at night, he told her with a grin. And she smiled back, for somehow in her mind, she apparently had decided to live again. As if the time after her injury had been a period of grieving, now she began a like time of healing.

Her hair became lustrous once more, gleaming as he brushed it twice daily. Her skin was again as porcelain, glowing in the candlelight at night when he put her into the bed. He left the candle lit for long moments every night, happy to lie beside her and watch her, tempted to press her for more than an occasional kiss, but he would not push her farther than he deemed it comfortable for her to progress.

And then one night, when he'd blown out the candle and she lay once again with her head on his shoulder, her hand reached to touch his face and she whispered a need he had not thought to hear from her lips.

"Simon, would you touch me?"

Chapter Fourteen

His heart seemed to stop beating, and his breath caught in his throat. "I am touching you, sweetheart," he said, drawing the words out in a casual fashion, his arm enclosing her, drawing her closer.

"Simon, don't be dense. I want you to *touch* me."

He thought her voice sounded snippish, as his mother would have said, and he laughed softly. "Was that an order, ma'am?"

She was unmoving beside him for a long moment. "Not unless you want it to be," she said finally.

"Where shall I begin, Grace? I fear you'll think me bold should I move your gown aside and brush your skin with my hand."

She laughed. No, it wasn't a laugh, he decided, but a giggle. Grace *giggled*.

And so he leaned over her, sliding her from her chosen spot on his shoulder, and his hand was very careful as he loosened the first four buttons on her gown. He'd helped her into that same gown only fifteen minutes earlier, for Grace had progressed to being almost dressed every day, wearing her robe and undergarments. But never in his dressing and undressing her had he touched any part of her body, but to smooth her garments in place.

Now he felt her breath hitch as the buttons came undone and he spread the bodice wide, revealing the upper slopes of her breasts. She'd gotten beyond a bandage, Belle telling her two weeks ago that the wound needed air to heal, and he'd found that Belle apparently possessed some great store of wisdom, for Grace did not argue with her.

Now, he leaned a bit closer and his fingertips touched the soft flesh there, where the fullness of her body became a woman's pride and a man's joy.

He felt her skin pebble beneath his fingertips and he looked at her quickly, meeting her gaze, but she only nodded a bit and waited.

For what he did not know. Could he go further, dare he uncover the skin that rose to a perfect pink bud that had hitherto delighted his eye? Perhaps, he thought. Perhaps she would let him see her, not just feel his hand against her skin.

And so he touched her more firmly, brushing back the gown a bit, revealing her breast to his eyes, almost to the soft pink crest. And there he paused, waiting. For what, he knew not, but again he waited for a word of guidance.

And it came. "Touch me, Simon. Please."

There was no need to ask twice, for he had hungered for just such a moment. For over a month, nearing two, he had ached to hold her curves in his hands, to love her as a husband would. And now she was willing to allow his touch. For more than that he would not ask. Not tonight. But she had given him leave, and so he pushed the gown lower and slid his hand beneath her breast, the left one, the uninjured side, for he feared she might flinch if he touched her right breast, there where cruel mouth and teeth had bruised and torn her flesh.

He bent over her and his lips kissed her with consummate care, at first only pressing his mouth against the soft skin, leaving the pink crest to tighten and pearl into a tempting berry. And then he opened his mouth, his lips and tongue aching to feel that small bit of flesh against them.

He bent to her, his lips barely brushing her skin. "Tell me if it's too much, sweetheart. I won't hurt you."

A small laugh escaped her lips. "Oh, Simon.

I know that. But you're making me ache. I need you. Please. Not like it was before, but just to let me know you still want me."

He groaned and his mouth closed over her, his tongue touching with delicate movements against the place where he had been wont to suckle and draw the tender flesh into his mouth. "All right?" he asked, his voice husky, the ache in his loins almost unbearable now.

"Oh, yes." Her sigh was long and sweet, and she held him there, her hand on his head, lifting his free hand to her mouth, blessing it with soft touches of teeth and lips and tongue.

He lifted from her and she seemed to withdraw. "You don't want to touch me where he…where he hurt me, do you?"

"Sweetheart, don't ever think that. I just don't want to upset you or frighten you. I'm aching to touch you everywhere I can reach on your body, but I won't do anything to cause you distress."

She met his gaze and frowned. "I'm distressed right now, Simon."

"Then stop me if you don't like what I'm doing, Grace." He took a deep breath and wished for a long moment that he had some female to speak with, some motherly soul who would know all the answers there were to understanding a wife. For at this moment, he was at sea and his boat was leaking.

With agile fingers, he undid the buttons beyond her waist, and then lay the bodice even wider, exposing both of her breasts, watching as they changed before his eyes, the crests puckering even more, the flesh becoming taut and full. He leaned to her, his mouth careful, and he kissed her again, opened his mouth against her flesh and drew in small increments against his tongue. He moved to the right breast, uncovering it completely, lifting it to see the healed place where the cruel, open wound had caused her such pain, and blessed the scarred spot with his tongue.

His hand held her rounded breast higher, exposing the tender underside, and he kissed her there. First one side, then the other, and he used his skill, learned at her side, during weeks past, giving her the pleasure he knew she'd enjoyed in the early days of their marriage. Finally he suckled gently at the tender place where one day his son might take nourishment from his mother.

"Simon. Simon." It seemed she could only speak his name and that in a hushed whisper that brought chills to run the length of his backbone.

"I love you, Grace. As no other man has ever loved a woman, I love you."

"And how many women have you loved?" she asked, her eyes teasing him.

"None before you, love. And only you for the rest of my life, and perhaps beyond."

"I knew that. I just wanted to hear you say it." She spoke solemnly, as though some great and mysterious event had occurred. And perhaps it had, he thought. For his wife had accepted his touch, had allowed him to love her as a husband, and should she so desire, he might soon be offered the privilege of taking her body once more as his own.

Of owning her freshness, the sweetness of her woman's flesh, the scent of her feminine being. And for that he was willing to wait, until she should open herself to him and asking him to cover her, offer him the gift of her love.

It was a day of celebration, an afternoon of pure happiness when Grace said she would like to sit with him on the swing. He deemed her strong enough, helped her with her underthings and dress, then put soft slippers on her feet. With her hand on his arm, he led her from the front door to sit beside him on the green swing.

She inhaled deeply of the air, sitting in the shadow of the porch roof, the September sun shining in unmatched brilliance, for her joy in the day was complete. Simon by her side, the sound of a horse passing on the road in front of the house, the shout of children at play nearby. There was a feeling of normalcy, a sense of the commonplace about this day, and she rejoiced that it should be so.

Happy that the pain and horror of her ordeal had passed, her body was healed, her heart well on its way and Simon was beside her, his warmth sustaining her.

A horse stopped by the gate and a man lifted himself from the saddle. *Uncle Joe,* her silent heart cried, and she smiled as he made his way to the porch, lifting a hand in greeting, then allowing his gaze to meet hers. Tired eyes touched upon her, a lined face seemed to gain new life as he watched her for a moment, and Joe drew closer, offering his hand.

She took it between her own, greeting him with an uplifted face, for she yearned for his kiss of greeting. She was not disappointed, for he bent and pressed his lips against her forehead, uttering soft words that told her of his concern for her.

Simon called out, his voice carrying from the porch into the house. "Ethel, would you bring some refreshments, please? Grace's uncle is here."

An answering sound of agreement reached their ears and Joe settled himself on a white, wooden chair that fit the body with a comfortable shape.

"Things are pretty much back to normal out at the ranch," he told Grace. "The men all ask about you most every day, and I decided it was time to take a look for myself and see that you were feeling better."

That Simon had sent word for him to stop by,

that he thought Grace needed to speak with him, was not mentioned, for Joe was a smart man. And mending fences was a job better done with fore-thought. And today, he knew he had more than a mile of fences to repair before he could once more find peace between himself and his niece.

He leaned forward in his chair, his big hands hanging down between his knees, and his words were slow and precise. "I was wrong, Grace. I didn't take into account your feelings as I should have. I set Kenny Summers on you without recognizing his failings. He was not a kindly man to begin with, and not until I recognized the darker side of his nature, did I repent heartily of my actions.

"I thought you needed marriage, the stability of a man in your life, perhaps children to fulfill you as a woman, and I interfered where I should not have. I fear that Kenny somehow heard of your inheritance and sought it for himself. For had you married him, the money left to you by your folks would have become his."

"I didn't know there was much money left for I assumed it was used up with the funerals and all. And then you took care of me, Uncle Joe. I had no idea there was anything left over until you told Simon before the wedding," Grace said.

Joe looked into her eyes and his own were dark with the pain of acknowledging his own poor judg-ment. "Can you ever forgive me, dear child, for my neglect of you? I miss you so dreadfully, your sweet smile and your gentle ways. You're so much like your mother, and it helped me deal with her loss while you were with me."

Grace knew that tears were close, and so she spoke quickly, lest she not be able to give him the answer she knew he deserved. "We were both wrong, Uncle Joe. For I was impatient with you and didn't express my feelings well. I would give much to live over those days I spent with you, but given the circumstances, I can only vow that my future will hold a closer relationship with you."

Joe caught Simon's eye. "I'm just thankful that Grace is safe and all is well here," Joe said.

Grace looked up then at Simon and her smile was warm. "I think we have much to be thankful for, not only my returning health, but the welcome we will be preparing for a new member of our household."

As she spoke, Ethel came out the door and a chuckle was heard from her direction. "Land sakes, I thought the child would never catch on to what's been happening in her own body. Guess she figured it out finally, Simon."

And his returned laughter verified her statement. Grace knew she looked smug, for she had held the knowledge deep within her for more than a week or so, recognizing that her body was far from regular in its rhythm, that she had not had a monthly cycle in more than two months, since before things had gone so badly awry. At first she'd blamed it on the illness that had wrought such havoc, and then had begun counting days and weeks and knew that there was more afoot.

Simon grinned at her. "Well, I'd hoped to speak with you without an audience, Grace, but Joe is family, after all, and who better to hear firsthand of our happiness?"

Joe beamed, his chest expanding at the news. "If I'm hearing things aright, I'll have to say I'm pleased as punch, Simon. And I'm happy for you, Grace, for this is what I knew would complete your life. I was not able to have a family of my own, and when you came to live at my place, I'd hoped you would take the place a daughter might have filled."

"I'm still available, Uncle Joe," she said quietly, her hand reaching for his. Their palms met and he curled her fingers within his grasp, his eyes warm upon her face.

"Can we celebrate a bit?" Ethel asked, motioning to the tray she'd carried out, a pitcher of lemonade lined up with four glasses. Lemon cake was set beside them, its glaze glistening moistly, for the tender treat was freshly out of the oven, and she'd sliced it quickly at Simon's summons.

The cake was soon gone, the lemonade glasses emptied, and with reluctance, Joe took his leave.

"I'll be back soon, and if you don't mind. I'd like to let the men out at the ranch know of your happiness, Grace. They've been most concerned about your welfare, and knowing that things are going well for you will be a bonus."

"Of course," she said, her smile tiring, but still brilliant. As Joe took his leave, Simon pulled Grace over, lifting her to his lap and cuddling her close as he set the swing in motion once more.

"Do you remember the day we were married, when we sat here together?" he asked softly, the words whispered against her temple.

She nodded, leaning against him fully, feeling the warmth of his body and the security of his arms sheltering her. "Umm…I was happy then, Simon. But not nearly as filled with joy as I am now. Then I was a girl, now I'm a woman. Then I was but a bride, and now I'm a wife. Your wife, and that satisfies me beyond all measure."

He held her slender form securely, his head bowing to press kisses upon her forehead and the soft line of her cheek. "I love you, Grace. More than any woman has ever been loved, I love you."

She was content, and in her contentment, she nestled against him, caught up in his embrace, secure in his love.

"You make me happy, Grace," he said simply.

"My mama used to tell me that each of us is responsible for finding our own happiness in life.

You're happy with me because you choose to be so, Simon. You made that choice many months ago, when you asked me to marry you. And you've set your course ever since. It's no surprise that you've found contentment with me."

"More than that, Grace. More than contentment, more than the happiness we've found holds us together. For we share a bond that is rare. We are joined in such a way that no evil can harm us, no outside force can rend the bond between us."

Now she spoke again, and before him a doorway stood open, for she offered him words he had not expected to hear. "I've not been much of a wife to you for a long time, Simon. I've failed you in that department of late, and it's time to make up for my failings. I want you to know that my arms ache to hold you and my body is empty without the knowledge of your love to sustain me. I need you, Simon. Perhaps more than at any time during our marriage."

He felt the darkness that lived within him shatter and begin to fade, as the light of Grace's smile was his once more. When he would have caught her up in an embrace, she stopped him, her hand on his chest, her fingers holding him in place. For she was not finished and he called on patience to infuse him.

Her words were a whisper. "Knowing that we will have a child has helped to dissolve the cage

I've lived in for so long. I want to come out, into your arms and into your heart."

His hands gripped hers and he held them against his chest, there where his heart pounded so rapidly. "You've always been in my heart, dear one. But if you feel you can offer yourself to me as a wife, if the time has come for that to happen between us, you know that I am more than ready."

He lifted her then, rose with her in his arms and carried her within the house, up the stairs and into their bedroom. Lowering himself to the side of the mattress, he held her closely, his embrace a warmth and security she seemed to welcome. She looked up at him and the light of love offered and accepted shone between them. In mere moments he took her clothing from her and helped her slide her sleeping gown over her head, placing her gently in the center of the bed, tugging a sheet up to cover her, as if he knew and understood her need for modesty.

Twilight filled the room, and but for the single candle he'd lit, lit so smoothly she had not been aware of his intent, it was shadowed in the room. The darkness fell swiftly as it was wont to do and Grace watched as Simon rose from the bed. He dropped his clothing to the floor, undressing quickly, then came to her and bent to the candle on the table beside the bed. "Shall I blow it out? Or leave it lit, Grace?"

She scooted down, her head on the pillow, her

body beneath the sheet. "So long as the curtain is drawn over the window, leave the candle lit. I truly don't mind if all of our imperfections are exposed by candlelight, for surely the glow will soften and make us appear perfect, each to the other."

"You are perfect to my eyes," he said, slipping beneath the sheet to hold her in his arms.

"Have I ever told you how handsome I thought you were, the first day we met?" she asked with a smile, recalling that day.

"No, but we have all night, sweetheart. You go on ahead and let me know just what you thought of me."

She met his smile and pushed against his shoulder with a closed fist. "I fear I'll make you too proud if you find out how much you appealed to the feminine part of me that day. Your shoulders were so broad, your hair so dark, your arms so strong as you held me there on the ground by the side of the road. It was as if you were my hero, my very own knight come to the rescue. And I absolutely basked in the warmth you offered me."

Simon remembered, and his words were soft. "I thought that even with the marks on your skin, your torn clothing and the violence done you that day, you were the most beautiful woman I'd ever seen. I knew I wanted you as I'd never wanted another girl in my life. That somehow I would teach you to care for me and would pray for the day I might make you my wife."

She laughed and brushed her kiss against his hand. "It seems we were on the same track then, from the very first, Simon. For it wasn't long until I knew you were the most important man ever to cross my path, that I was willing to live my life at your side, if you would but ask me."

He eased her closer, not wanting to frighten her with the ardor he kept under control, but needing her warmth. "I've come to appreciate the Blackwoods more and more in the past weeks and months. They seem to feel that they're a part of our little family, Grace."

"They will be almost like grandparents to our child, won't they?" she asked.

"Indeed, our baby will have relatives aplenty, for Ethel has plans already for claiming him or her as a grandbaby, and your uncle will be on hand, I'll guarantee. Along with my parents and the Blackwoods, you'll have family in every nook and cranny of your life, Grace."

"I can't tell you how that makes me feel. For when my parents died and I was left alone, with but my uncle to help me, I felt so lost, bereft perhaps. As if I were walking a solitary path, for Uncle Joe and I barely had time to form any sort of relationship before things began to happen and we were torn apart."

"You'll never be alone again, I promise you."
And as if he would seal that promise with more
than kisses, he pushed her gently to her back and
rose over her, his body covering hers with the
warmth of a man set on being a husband in every
sense of the word.

She looked up at him with no trace of fear in her
eyes, no sense of apprehension in her touch as she
held him in a close embrace. "I asked the doctor
about this, Simon, and he assured me that making
love with my husband would not harm our child
in any way. So long as you are careful and don't
get…*rambunctious*, is the word he used, then all
should be well."

"Rambunctious, he said? Well, I'll do my best
to be circumspect and formal in this endeavor,
ma'am."

His teasing tones made her laugh for she knew
the depths of Simon's passion, the desire for fulfillment he was capable of arousing in her body, and
she did not fear his careless use of her.

"It seems I've been waiting for this longer than
I could bear. I've wanted to take you, fill you with
my need and give you pleasure again."

She laughed up at him, her eyes alight, and he
thought again of how very blessed he was to have
her here. In his life and in his bed.

He leaned closer to her, holding himself from
her body a bit, for he would not make her feel

trapped by the weight of his form. His mouth was drawn to the lips beneath his, the silken skin of her face and throat, and the promise of curves that drew his eyes with such audacity. For she knew well how to tempt him, and as he watched, she slipped her fingers between her buttons and undid the bodice of her gown, exposing the rounding of her breasts to his gaze.

She was as needy as he, it seemed, for she showed every sign of wanting this joining, of craving the touch of his body against and within her own. Her legs parted and she made room for him, scooting her gown higher, so that his flesh touched hers, his manhood pressed for entry against the soft folds that hid the feminine part of her.

"I should have shaved again," he murmured, knowing he would leave marks on her fragile skin.

"I like to feel your whiskers. It lets me know you're a man and you need me. I want you to always need me in just this way, Simon." She curved against him, and he knew a moment of hesitation as he would have slipped within her silken sheath, had he not shifted just a bit.

"Simon…I don't want to wait," she whispered.

"Are you sure? You'll tell me if—"

Her words overrode his, her voice certain and sure. "Simon. Just love me. Now, before I burst with wanting you."

And so he did, with all the skill his masculine body could call forth. Tenderly, carefully, lest he bring her a moment of discomfort, he loved her. His hands held her close, his mouth somehow found her breasts, even as his lower body sought out the depths of her most tender places. And she lifted to him, her soft cries and sighs of pleasure rising as music to his ears. They loved as if they had never known such bliss, such happiness before, and perhaps it was so, for a new depth of joy overshadowed all that had come to pass before this time.

And when at last the candle guttered in its holder, when the moon had risen and shed its light into the room where two lovers slept, there was a peaceful hush that filled the room, indeed the whole house. For Simon and Grace had overcome obstacles and diversity and had faced harsh circumstances with a unity of spirit that seemed rare and beautiful. And so, they slept, perhaps to dream. Simon of the woman he held, Grace recalling the memory of the day he had come to her rescue, saving her from further harm.

For surely he had saved her that day, claimed her as his own. And as he'd told her later on, he'd devoted himself to the task he'd undertaken—that of saving Grace.

* * * * *

COMING NEXT MONTH FROM

HARLEQUIN®
HISTORICAL

Available June 28, 2011

REQUEST YOUR FREE BOOKS!

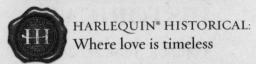

HARLEQUIN® HISTORICAL:
Where love is timeless

2 FREE NOVELS PLUS 2 **FREE GIFTS!**

YES! Please send me 2 FREE Harlequin® Historical novels and my 2 FREE gifts (gifts are worth about $10). After receiving them, if I don't wish to receive any more books, I can return the shipping statement marked "cancel." If I don't cancel, I will receive 6 brand-new novels every month and be billed just $4.94 per book in the U.S. or $5.49 per book in Canada. That's a savings of at least 18% off the cover price! It's quite a bargain! Shipping and handling is just 50¢ per book in the U.S. and 75¢ per book in Canada.* I understand that accepting the 2 free books and gifts places me under no obligation to buy anything. I can always return a shipment and cancel at any time. Even if I never buy another book from the Reader Service, the two free books and gifts are mine to keep forever.

246/349 HDN FC45

Name   (PLEASE PRINT)

Address   Apt. #

City   State/Prov.   Zip/Postal Code

Signature (if under 18, a parent or guardian must sign)

Mail to the **Reader Service:**
IN U.S.A.: P.O. Box 1867, Buffalo, NY 14240-1867
IN CANADA: P.O. Box 609, Fort Erie, Ontario L2A 5X3
Not valid for current subscribers to Harlequin Historical books.

Want to try two free books from another line?
Call 1-800-873-8635 or visit www.ReaderService.com.

* Terms and prices subject to change without notice. Prices do not include applicable taxes. N.Y. residents add applicable sales tax. Canadian residents will be charged applicable taxes. Offer not valid in Quebec. This offer is limited to one order per household. All orders subject to credit approval. Credit or debit balances in a customer's account(s) may be offset by any other outstanding balance owed by or to the customer. Please allow 4 to 6 weeks for delivery. Offer available while quantities last.

Your Privacy—The Reader Service is committed to protecting your privacy. Our Privacy Policy is available online at www.ReaderService.com or upon request from the Reader Service.

We make a portion of our mailing list available to reputable third parties that offer products we believe may interest you. If you prefer that we not exchange your name with third parties, or if you wish to clarify or modify your communication preferences, please visit us at www.ReaderService.com/consumerchoice or write to us at Reader Service Preference Service, P.O. Box 9062, Buffalo, NY 14269. Include your complete name and address.

HH11

USA TODAY *bestselling author B.J. Daniels*
takes you on a trip to Whitehorse, Montana,
and the Chisholm Cattle Company.

RUSTLED

Available July 2011 from Harlequin Intrigue.

As the dust settled, Dawson got his first good look at the rustler. A pair of big Montana sky-blue eyes glared up at him from a face framed by blond curls.

A woman rustler?

"You have to let me go," she hollered as the roar of the stampeding cattle died off in the distance.

"So you can finish stealing my cattle? I don't think so." Dawson jerked the woman to her feet.

She reached for the gun strapped to her hip hidden under her long barn jacket.

He grabbed the weapon before she could, his eyes narrowing as he assessed her. "How many others are there?" he demanded, grabbing a fistful of her jacket. "I think you'd better start talking before I tear into you."

She tried to fight him off, but he was on to her tricks and pinned her to the ground. He was suddenly aware of the soft curves beneath the jean jacket she wore under her coat.

"You have to listen to me." She ground out the words from between her gritted teeth. "You have to let me go. If you don't they will come back for me and they will kill you. There are too many of them for you to fight off alone. You won't stand a chance and I don't want your blood on my hands."

"I'm touched by your concern for me. Especially after you just tried to pull a gun on me."

"I wasn't going to shoot you."

Dawson hauled her to her feet and walked her the rest of the way to his horse. Reaching into his saddlebag, he pulled out a length of rope.

"You can't tie me up."

He pulled her hands behind her back and began to tie her wrists together.

"If you let me go, I can keep them from coming back," she said. "You have my word." She let out an unladylike curse. "I'm just trying to save your sorry neck."

"And I'm just going after my cattle."

"Don't you mean your boss's cattle?"

"Those cattle are mine."

"*You're* a Chisholm?"

"Dawson Chisholm. And you are…?"

"Everyone calls me Jinx."

He chuckled. "I can see why."

Bronco busting, falling in love…it's all in a day's work.
Look for the rest of their story in

RUSTLED

Available July 2011 from Harlequin Intrigue
wherever books are sold.

THE NOTORIOUS
WOLFES

**A powerful dynasty,
where secrets and scandal never sleep!**

Eight siblings, blessed with wealth, but denied the one thing they wanted—a father's love. Haunted by their past and driven to succeed, the Wolfes scattered to the far corners of the globe. It's said that even the blackest of souls can be healed by the purest of love....

But can the dynasty rise again?

Beginning July 2011

A NIGHT OF SCANDAL—*Sarah Morgan*
THE DISGRACED PLAYBOY—*Caitlin Crews*
THE STOLEN BRIDE—*Abby Green*
THE FEARLESS MAVERICK—*Robyn Grady*
THE MAN WITH THE MONEY—*Lynn Raye Harris*
THE TROPHY WIFE—*Janette Kenny*
THE GIRL THAT LOVE FORGOT—*Jennie Lucas*
THE LONE WOLFE—*Kate Hewitt*

8 volumes to collect and treasure!

♣ Harlequin®

SPECIAL EDITION

Life, Love and Family

THE TEXANS ARE COMING!

Reader-favorite miniseries Montana Mavericks
is back in Special Edition with new loves,
adventures and more.

July 2011 features *USA TODAY* bestselling author
CHRISTINE RIMMER
with
RESISTING MR. TALL, DARK & TEXAN.

A Texas oil mogul arrives in Thunder Canyon on
business and soon falls for his personal assistant. Only
one problem—she's

Can he convinc

Fi

L
Montana Maveri
in eac

August
November

Available w